Why Children Misbehave

AND WHAT TO DO ABOUT IT

Christine Adams, Ph.D.   Ernest Frugé, Ph.D.

New Harbinger Publications, Inc.

Publisher's Note

This publication is designed to provide accurate and authoritative information in regard to the subject matter covered. It is sold with the understanding that the publisher is not engaged in rendering pyschological, financial, legal, or other professional services. If expert assistance or counseling is needed, the services of a competent professional should be sought.

Copyright © 1996 Christine Adams, Ph.D., and Ernest Frugé, Ph.D.
New Harbinger Publications, Inc.
5674 Shattuck Avenue
Oakland, CA 94609

Cover design by SHELBY DESIGNS & ILLUSTRATES.

Photo credit: John Everett: Cover, pp. 7, 19, 21, 29, 53, 75, 86. Janice Adams: pp. 5, 75, 78, 131, 136, 156. All other photos by Christine Adams and Ernest Frugé.

Distributed in U.S.A. primarily by Publishers Group West; in Canada by Raincoast Books; in Great Britain by Airlift Book Company, Ltd.; in South Africa by Real Books, Ltd.; in Australia by Boobook; and in New Zealand by Tandem Press.

Library of Congress Catalog Card Number: 96-67939

ISBN 1-57224-051-2 paperback

First printing 1996, 8,000 copies

This book is dedicated to our children and our parents. They have taught us the most fundamental lessons about human relationships. The book is also dedicated to all the children and parents who strive to improve their relationships.

Contents

Preface

You will not find quick fixes or shortcuts offered in this book. There are none. What you will find is support for and reassurance about the rewarding but commonly difficult and frustrating task of parenting children.

This book describes some ways of approaching discipline that are flexible but consistent. Discipline means teaching and learning. Effective discipline teaches children how to gain control over their behavior, to adapt to demands of life, and to appreciate the rights and needs of others. These methods are not new fads, but are the tried and true methods that forty years of research on child development has shown to be the most effective ways of disciplining children.

These methods work because they maintain your authority and leadership as the parent while allowing you to build a positive, close relationship with your child. With these methods, you, the parent, will teach your child self-control, consideration for others, and self-respect through your own actions.

The best parenting methods are ones that continually send the messages of love and respect for oneself and others. These methods take some time to show results, but they make discipline more effective because they lead children to feel valued and to appreciate the benefits of doing the right thing.

Finding the best methods of parenting is like establishing a healthy lifestyle. It takes time, planning, and self-discipline to carry out and often takes longer to show positive results. However, the results are usually more enduring and lead to more friendly and pleasant day-to-day relationships within the family as a whole.

THE BIG PICTURE

CHAPTER 1

Understanding Aggression

Key Ideas

- Anger and aggression are normal but need to be controlled and appropriately channeled.

- Children learn to control their aggression when they see adults control their own aggressive drives.

- Children need to learn how to balance their needs with the needs of others.

Important Definitions

1. **Survival instinct:** Natural tendencies to protect yourself and your loved ones; also the motivation to use talents, compete, and achieve a better life.

2. **Aggression:** Hostile or harmful action taken to satisfy your needs or goals without regard for the rights of others.

3. **Assertiveness:** Constructive use of the survival instinct to achieve a positive goal. Assertive actions are taken to advance one's own interests and to protect one's rights; they are not taken to infringe upon the rights of others. Assertive actions are respectful of the rights of both yourself and others.

When children are frustrated, they may behave aggressively.

Survival Instinct

You are born with a survival instinct that helps you take care of yourself and your loved ones. This survival instinct is necessary for a healthy adaptation to life's stresses and challenges. Without it, you would not succeed in life. You would never try to do anything. You would never take on challenges, strive to better yourself, or fight for your rights.

Most of the time, the survival instinct is directed into positive goals and outlets. Examples of this positive, constructive use of the survival instinct include the following: self-defense, healthy competition, courageous acts, leadership, and achievement of personal goals (education, sports, career, social causes, and so on).

learning

sports

The survival instinct helps us reach positive goals.

The word assertiveness is now commonly used to describe this positive use of the survival instinct for nonharmful, constructive goals. Sometimes people use the word aggressive to describe something positive, such as aggressive medical treatment or aggressively going after business, but they are actually describing self-defense, or assertiveness.

To get along in the world, children have to learn how to balance their own needs and wants with the needs of other people. Successful children know constructive ways of handling their angry and aggressive feelings. They understand that being cooperative yet assertive helps them find that balance between themselves and others.

Successful children balance their needs with the needs of others.

When the survival instinct is not controlled, the result can be harmful or hurtful behavior, which is aggression. In this book, the word aggression means harmful or hurtful behavior which can be either intentional or unintentional. Aggressive feelings and behaviors are a natural part of human nature. However, the price of uncontrolled aggression for children, families, and society is enormous. Learning to control aggression is one of the central challenges every child and parent face.

Aggression is normal but needs to be controlled.

Learning to Control Aggressiveness

Your child will be motivated to learn how to control aggressiveness and to cooperate when he or she feels loved and valued by you and other important adults. Your child will also learn to control aggressiveness when important adults in his or her life control their own aggressiveness. Children imitate what they see; when important adults behave aggressively in response to frustration, children tend to follow that example. However, when you show self-control and respect toward your child when he or she is misbehaving, your child learns to value respectful, constructive resolution of conflict. Your child also sees that people who love each other can express strong disagreements but still behave with consideration and respect.

Most of the time, young children do not really want to hurt others when they behave aggressively. Their aggressiveness is usually motivated by a desire to get something they want or is a natural response to frustration. Children do not automatically outgrow aggressiveness. If children continue to get what they want enough of the time by being aggressive or if they themselves are treated aggressively, they tend to become more and more aggressive as they get older.

Self-Protection Is Necessary

While you want your child to be cooperative, sometimes aggression is necessary for self-protection. You do not want your child to be selfish or a bully, but neither do you want your child to be pushed around or intimidated by others. Parents certainly want children to know when to rightly question the authority of adults and older children so that they can protect themselves from strangers or dangerous situations.

The best way to teach your child to judge these situations accurately is to keep the parent-child relationship close and trustworthy. Parenting methods that emphasize understanding with reasonable, predictable standards of conduct foster closeness and trust. Using methods that focus exclusively on controlling misbehavior by demanding submission is a mistake because these methods miss the more important, larger goals of teaching children self-control, independent thinking, problem-solving, and compassion for others.

Aggression is necessary for self-protection.

CHAPTER 2

Guidance

Key Ideas

- Being empathic and understanding helps children calm down and behave.

- Understanding the normal stages of child development makes it easier to step back from the heat of the moment and use an empathic approach.

- Limits or restrictions on behavior need to be predictable and consistent.

- Being either too permissive or too harsh is harmful to children.

- Using an empathic, problem-solving approach is better in the long run because this approach emphasizes teaching children what to do.

Important Definitions

1. **Empathy:** Being able to see and understand things from another person's view and to imagine what it feels like to be in that person's shoes. Empathy is *not* sympathy or simple reassurance. Empathy does not necessarily mean agreeing with someone.

2. **Limit:** A restriction on behavior. Examples of limits include:

   - Rules—*Muddy shoes stay outside.*
   - Boundaries around acceptable behavior—*Whispering is acceptable in the library, loud talking is not.*
   - Standards of conduct—*Be polite to others.*

3. **Consequence:** A consequence is any result or effect that follows after or because of an action. A consequence can be either positive or negative. In parenting, consequences can be used to encourage desirable behavior or to discourage misbehavior. Consequences can happen naturally, accidentally, or be delivered intentionally by a parent: Examples include:

   - Getting a failing grade because of not doing school work
   - Increasing skill level because of sufficient practice
   - Not getting dessert if dinner was not eaten
   - Cleaning up a mess or spill that one has made
   - Having a toy taken away after it has been thrown at someone
   - Being praised for doing a good deed

A consequence can also be something parents *do not* do, such as permit a child to spend the night with a friend. Parents can enforce limits by using consequences.

> *When parents establish reasonable rules, react to distress with empathy and firm limits, and back limits up with appropriate, consistent consequences, then over time their children develop clear expectations and learn that cooperation is more advantageous in the long run.*

4. **Limit-setting:** Putting restrictions on behavior through the use of clear consequences. In limit-setting, consequences are what parents do or do not do in response to their child's behavior. Examples include:

   - "You can run outside but you must walk inside the house. If you run in the house, you will not be allowed to play."
   - "If you keep arguing with me, you will need to go to your room for fifteen minutes to calm down."

   Consistency in limit-setting is very important because children's expectations are based on the pattern of limits set by parents. Children will behave according to what they expect will happen.

5. **Empathic limit-setting:** Combines understanding and acceptance of how a child feels and thinks with a consistent, reasonable restriction on what that child is allowed to do and a logical consequence for the child's misbehavior. Empathic limit-setting means that a child's feelings and perspective are considered while rules are enforced.

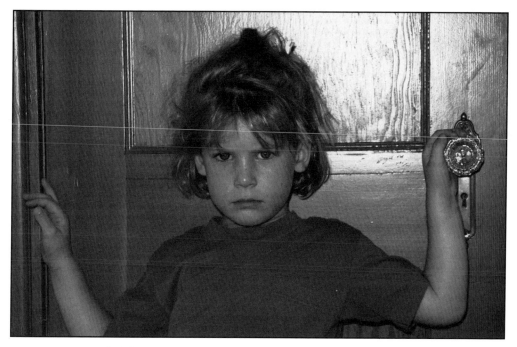

Children need reasonable rules and compassion.

Children Respond Better When They Feel Understood

When you are accepting and understanding about how your child feels, your child will be more easily redirected to appropriate activities and guided to better ways of handling upset feelings. You will get the best results when you are understanding and firm without being irritable or excessively angry. Over time, when you control your own temper and show some understanding, your child will listen better and calm down sooner. This is because children respond better to limits and restrictions when they know their parents respect their feelings. Children can also see how disagreements and problems can be handled without family members getting too upset. This combination of understanding and setting clear, firm limits on behavior is called *empathic limit-setting*.

Children respond well to empathic limit-setting.

Examples of Parent Empathic Limit-Setting for Preschool-Age Children

Situation: Child fussing about not getting to wear what she or he wants to wear to school or day care.

Examples of parent empathic statements:

- "I know this is your favorite shirt."
- "You're angry with me because I won't let you wear your favorite shirt."
- "It's hard for you when you don't get your way."
- "You don't like me to say no."

Examples of parent limit-setting statements:

- "The weather is too cold for you to wear this shirt; you might get sick. If you can calm yourself down, you can pick out (choose) a cold-weather shirt to wear today."
- "You need to get back in control by the time I count to three or you will go to time-out."
- "You need to put on the clothes I picked out or you will not get to watch TV this morning (or some other privilege)."
- "If you keep fussing, we will not have time to stop at (special place child likes) before (or after) school today because fussing takes up the time we could be spending there."
- "If you cannot cooperate about getting dressed, then you will not get the privilege of choosing what you will wear for one day."

Examples of combining these into empathic limit-setting statements:

- "I know this is your favorite shirt. It's too cold outside for you to wear it today. I know you're upset about it, but you will be too cold if you wear it. You need to pick out a cold-weather shirt. If you do it now, you'll have time to watch a little TV before school."
- (With continued refusal): "I'm going to count to three and if you are still fussing after I get to three, you will not get to watch TV this morning (or after school)."

Handling Problems and Shifting Gears

Limit-setting can also be used to teach your child how to handle problems and how to shift gears or redirect him- or herself. Here are some examples.

Empathy	Limit-Setting	Problem-Solving and Redirecting
"I know you want that toy and you are angry . . .	. . . but it's not OK to grab it out of Mark's hands."	1. "You can ask him to share or let you use it when he's done." 2. "You need to find another toy." 3. "What could you do instead?"
"I know that toy looks like the one you have at home . . .	. . . but this toy belongs to the school and Mark is using it now."	1. "Let's ask Mark to let you play with it when he's done." 2. "Let's find another toy that you don't get to play with at home."
"I know you are tired and miss your Mom and Dad . . .	. . . it's OK to be sad / angry but it's not OK to whine because it upsets you and other people."	"Let's find something that will help you feel better while you are here. How about. . . ."
"I know it was your turn on the swing . . .	. . . but you need to tell me what the problem is in a regular, calm voice instead of crying / whining, so I can understand you."	"Let's go talk to Mary about what she did and work this out."
"I know you want to do things for yourself . . .	. . . but you cannot climb up the shelves to get toys. It's not safe."	"You need to come get me (or other adult) when you need something high up."

Examples of Parent Empathic Limit-Setting for Elementary-Age Children

Situation 1: Kids being rowdy to the point of being out of control.

At the time of the misbehavior:

- "Look guys. I know you are all excited about getting to spend the night together. You all are getting too loud and rowdy.
  I can't get to sleep and I'm worried that one of you is going to get hurt or something's going to get broken. You all need to quiet down, stay in your sleeping bags, and start getting yourselves to sleep.
  I expect everyone to be a good friend and help the others stay quiet. If you all want to spend the night together again soon, you need to show me you can settle yourselves down, not disturb me, and get to sleep."

After the incident has already occurred:

- "Last night, you and your friends were too loud and rowdy.
  I had to keep coming in your room and reminding you to quiet down and get to sleep. I know you get excited when you have friends over, but when you are loud like that, I can't get enough sleep.
  If you want to have your friends spend the night again, all of you will have to be in your room and quiet by 10:30 PM. If I have to come in after 10:30, then you will not get to have anyone spend the night for several weeks and you will not get to spend the night at anyone else's house either."

Situation 2: Child refuses to get schoolwork organized on time.

- "Lisa, I know you were very busy today and practice took longer than usual, but you still need to get your schoolwork finished and in your bookbag now. I'll help you tonight if you need me, but I'm not going to be running around tomorrow morning looking for your stuff when we're all trying to get ready for work and school. If your schoolwork is not in your bag when it's time to leave you will just have to go to school without it."

Situation 3: Child brings the wrong show-and-tell item to school.

- "I can understand that you'd be upset and embarrassed. What do you think you can do the next time so this won't happen again?"

Situation 4: Child is complaining about not getting to watch more TV after allotted TV time is used up. Child begins to argue that all of his or her friends watch more TV than he or she gets to watch. The larger theme is that the child is insisting on more privileges because *everyone else* has more privileges.

- "I know it seems like everyone else gets to watch TV more than you and maybe a lot of kids do. I know you're disappointed and mad. The rule in our house is that you only get to watch TV for a little bit after your homework is done and a little bit on weekends.

    If there is a special show on that would be good for you to watch, you can ask us and maybe you can watch that special program. If you keep arguing with me about this, I won't let you watch any TV for two days."

Child continues to argue for expanded privileges. Giving the child a cue or warning about the problem behavior is appropriate and helpful to the child:

- "You are still arguing with me about it. I've told you that if you keep arguing then you will lose your TV privileges for two days. This is your last warning. If you ask to watch more TV tonight, I won't let you watch TV for two days. That's enough, now."

Sometimes your child will continue to argue and test limits after they are set and enforced. This testing of the limits is very irritating, but developmentally necessary and appropriate. You may be tempted to simply increase the restriction by adding to the time your child cannot watch TV. Try not to fall into this cycle. At this point, the situation has gone beyond frustration about not getting to watch TV to challenging your authority to limit your child's behavior in general. You need to shift from setting limits for a specific incident to teaching your child how to accept a limit and maintain self-control when he or she is frustrated instead of becoming more and more demanding.

- "OK, I warned you that if you kept on arguing you'd lose your TV privileges. You may not watch TV for two days.
  I know you're mad, but I am not going to change my mind about the TV. If you keep on arguing, you're going to lose other privileges, not just TV privileges.
  Now we can talk about the reasons why we have this rule about TV if you want, but I don't want to talk to you when you're mad and when I'm mad. If you can't calm down, you'll need to go to your room until you're calm."

Protecting Positive Relationships

Combining empathy and understanding with clear, age-appropriate rules, limits, and restrictions on behavior reduces the overall amount of conflict between parent and child. Frequent conflicts tear relationships apart. Empathic limit-setting in response to misbehavior works to reduce conflict because empathy protects your child's self-esteem, while limits teach your child what to do and what not to do. Positive relationships are nurtured among family members because respect and self-discipline are modeled and encouraged. Children feel less discouraged and resentful.

Empathic limit-setting also sets an example of self-control and logical thinking about what to do instead of doing the misbehavior. When you combine empathy with clear limits on behavior, you support your child's healthy development because this provides a warm, secure, and emotionally safe environment. People can actually learn more from their mistakes than from their successes. An empathic, secure environment makes learning from mistakes as well as successes safe for children because they know their parents respect and value them even when they misbehave.

Running Wild Is Also Harmful

Harsh or humiliating discipline clearly has harmful effects on children, but letting children run wild without firm limit-setting and supervision is also harmful to them. When you are too permissive, your child can begin to feel entitled to get whatever he or she wants. Children may also learn that they can get what they want from others through intimidation. This will make it hard for them to have healthy relationships with others both as children and as adults. Children may tend to feel that their needs should come first and things should always go their way. They may also develop a deeper sense of insecurity and vulnerability because they do not know if their parents are capable of protecting them. For example, if a child can push around his or her parent, the child may begin to fear that the parent is too weak to protect the child from harm or even to make good decisions affecting the family and child. Children may get what they want materially or get to do what they want routinely, but a lack of active guidance from parents can lead them to feel fundamentally neglected and therefore worthless.

Lovable Children Can Also Be Very Irritating

Even lovable children are irritating and provocative from time to time. When the routine stresses of modern life are combined with a child's irritating and frustrating behavior, even devoted, patient parents can have difficulty controlling their own strong, emotional reactions. Under these pressures and circumstances, a parent can with good reason be so upset that thinking about the child's point of view and being understanding can be very hard. For example, typical toddlers have normal and necessary urges to be independent. These demands to do things for themselves can be very aggravating to a parent under time pressure, such as when the parent must be punctual to an appointment. Understanding the normal phases of child development will help you step back from the heat of the moment and think about your child's

Step back from the heat of the moment.

perspective before deciding what steps to take. Having accurate expectations of what children are able to do and not do at different ages plus knowing how children best learn new behavior is helpful. Planning ahead and preventing problems then becomes more straightforward and less difficult.

When parents understand the normal phases their children go through, corrections can be more helpful. For example, as children move from preschool age to elementary age, they become very concerned about being competent, that is, being knowledgeable and able to do things well.

Situation: Older child is worried about being thought of as dumb and incompetent. The older child puts down a younger sibling for not knowing something—"I have the stupidest little sister in the world!" A simple criticism of the older sibling could reinforce his or her concern about being dumb and incompetent. Instead of responding with a criticism of the older child, the parent might say something like the following:

- "I know how proud you are that you can do so many things well now. I'm proud of you, too. It's not okay to make fun of your sister because she can't do as many things as well as you. Four-year-olds don't know as much as eight-year-olds because they are younger and haven't had as much time to learn things. When you were four, you did not know what you know now. When your sister is eight like you, she will know what you know. You need to say you are sorry to her."

This type of response helps the parent keep focused on the larger, central rule being broken rather than just the specific incident. In the example above, the central rule being broken is *Do not put someone down for not having as much of something as you do.* The parent also wants to teach the child that the logical consequence of insulting someone is to make an apology. A response such as the one above, gives the parent an opportunity to practice what was preached. If the parent had simply criticized the older child, the situation could easily be seen as a double standard where adults can get away with criticizing and putting down children, but children are called on the carpet when they do the exact same thing.

Misbehavior in Public Is Embarrassing

Parents can also be embarrassed and get angry when their children misbehave in public. Although public displays of misbehavior from children are never pleasant, having accurate expectations of children may make these public displays of misbehavior a bit easier to tolerate. You may understandably feel embarrassed by your child's misbehavior in front of others. Sometimes this embarrassment comes from a concern about what other people think of your ability as a parent.

Actually, most bystanders are sympathetic because they know from experience how difficult it is to raise children. Bystanders who are critical are probably more concerned about being inconvenienced than they are about the healthy development of your child. Children and parents should not be criticized when children act their age even when it is annoying. After all, six-year-olds are not expected to learn geometry. Why then should a six-year-old be expected to have the emotional self-control of a child twice that age? Raising children is hard and stressful. Parents, like children, need more support than criticism.

Two Steps Forward, One Step Back

A child's emotional and social growth is slow and irregular, and normal immaturity can be very frustrating. Children often take two steps forward and one step back. Growing up and learning how to follow rules and accept disappointment takes more guidance from adults for a much longer period of time than parents probably like. Having fair expectations of your child and a sense of humor about the slow, irregular pace of growing up can help you take the steps back in stride and enjoy the steps forward all the more.

Two steps forward . . .

One step back

CHAPTER 3

Family Relationships

Key Ideas

- Parents are teachers and leaders.

- Positive relationships with important adults encourage healthy self-esteem and self-control.

- The quality of the parent-child relationship or relationships with other significant people is most important to a child's overall development.

- Parenting methods shape and maintain the quality of parent-child relationships.

- The difficult job of parenting is made easier when parents have a basic knowledge of child development and an understanding of how behavior is shaped and changed.

Important Definitions

1. **Self-esteem:** How a person feels about him or herself. Two basic components are feeling capable ("I can do things well") and feeling worthwhile ("I am loved and valued by others").

2. **Developmental level:** Children increase their ability in steps, or stages, as they grow and mature. Predictable levels of abilities are expected at different ages. For example, an infant is unable to speak words, but the typical five-year-old uses complex speech and language. The developmental level of a child is the age range that is usual for their level of ability.

3. **Discipline:** In parenting, discipline means to guide and educate children about how to live effectively in our world. Effective discipline emphasizes teaching children rather than punishing them.

Children go through predictable, normal stages.

What Kind of Person Will Your Child Be?

- What kind of person do you want your child to be as an adult?
- What kind of character do you want your child to develop?
- What qualities, values, and virtues do you admire and respect?

What kind of character will your child have?

Children are not born with values or a set personality. Their personal characteristics are influenced by their relationships with their families, important adults, and their communities, as well as by the examples set for them. Building and encouraging a good, solid character requires self-discipline from parents and a clear idea of their goals for their child's overall development. Having a good, solid character involves more than being an obedient person. People with good, solid characters show independent thinking, respect for self and others, and self-discipline even in the face of temptation.

Positive Parent-Child Relationships

The quality of the parent-child relationship (or relationships with other people who are important to the child) is vital to a child's complete development. Positive relationships with parents and other important adults encourage healthy self-esteem, self-control, and a solid character. When these relationships are positive and healthy, children want to learn how to cooperate and behave out of love for their parents and other significant persons in their lives.

Parenting methods shape the quality of this parent-child relationship. Methods that send the message of love and commitment to the child emphasize love and self-control for both parent and child. These methods must also help the child understand the impact of misbehavior on relationships and show the child that there are consistent consequences for misbehavior.

You and your child will benefit if you have a clear, long-term vision of what kind of adult you want your child to be. This long-term goal can help you be more consistent by focusing on the big picture instead of each misbehavior. A clear vision will help you choose consistent methods of discipline. Ask yourself:

- Is this method consistent with the values I want my child to have?
- When I use this method, does my behavior model the way I want my child to behave?
- Will this method teach my child how to be the adult I want him or her to become?

When each incident becomes less important than the overall direction, generally day-to-day tension occurs less often between parents and children.

There Are No Magic Tricks

While learning specific parenting techniques is helpful, these techniques are of little use unless they are a logical part of a larger, consistent vision that fits a child's developmental level and needs. Parents who have a basic knowledge of what children can do at different ages and a basic knowledge of how behavior is shaped and changed are better prepared to deal with the difficulties and frustrations of parenting.

These parents have reasonable expectations of their children and sufficient confidence about how to approach problems or potential problems. Don't beat yourself up for parenting mistakes—learn from them; you will be more able to plan ahead and prevent small troubles from becoming big troubles.

In addition to knowing specific techniques keep the following in mind:

1. Keep your expectations fair and reasonable. Many times, parents become frustrated because their expectations are too high or because they are unaware of the normal stages of development that all children go through. When parents know that toddlers practice independence by running off, not getting quite so angry when it happens is easier. Fair and reasonable expectations also help parents plan ahead to prevent problems.

2. Know that physical, mental, and emotional abilities develop at different rates within each individual child. Children frequently have the ability to know what is expected of them before they have developed enough emotional control over their impulses to perform correctly on a regular basis. Children need guidance more than criticism. Remember, also, that no two children are completely alike. What works with one child does not necessarily work with another.

3. Know how your child thinks and how he or she will view the world at different ages. For example, a three-year-old thinks the snail at the corner is the same snail from two blocks ago. Young children are normally self-centered and think mostly of themselves. Know what themes are important to children at different ages. Toddlers are striving for independence, preschoolers for mastery over basic life tasks, elementary-age children for good friendships, and adolescents for all of these things.

4. Be curious and thoughtful. This basically means that parents should stop, think, and honestly try to understand the reasons why their children behave the way they do. For example, a child might misbehave for many different reasons and each reason could require a different kind of response from a parent. Children might act aggressively or uncooperatively when they are feeling angry, scared, tired, or even physically ill. Look for what set off the problem behavior or what is motivating your child at that time. Sometimes the problem is as simple as your child misunderstanding words or routines that you take for granted.

Be a Teacher and a Leader

Parents who adopt a teaching attitude rather than a punishing attitude are more effective. A teaching attitude means that the parent tries to remember what the child needs to learn from any situation. A teaching attitude also means the parent considers what the child can reasonably be expected to know and remember without assistance from Mom or Dad. When you are in a teaching frame of mind, you can be calmer and less reactive. You can think about the problem behavior while keeping in mind the more important behavior to be taught, such as courtesy or respect. When you control your own anger, your child will learn to respect you and will want to try hard to follow your values and rules. Your child will also see you set an example of how to be in control even when angry.

Teach By Example

Children imitate the behavior they see. However, they can only see behavior through the eyes of a child. Their imitations are shaped and limited by their youthful view of the world. A common example is a child at play pretending to be an adult and scolding pets, dolls, or younger siblings in an exaggeration of a scolding she or he has previously received. Children will do what they see others do. If they are shamed or spanked, they are likely to shame or hit other children or animals. If parents routinely say "please," "thank you," and "you're welcome," so will their children. If parents respect their children's feelings, the children will learn to respect the feelings of others. If parents do not allow themselves to be taken advantage of, children will learn how to protect themselves from being used by others.

Parents who learn to apologize or admit a mistake when going against their own teachings find that their children learn to do the same. When you apologize and admit mistakes, you help your child discover that making mistakes is normal instead of disastrous. You can teach your child that although mistakes can be painful, mistakes can also be useful ways of learning rules, skills, and how to get along in the world. Under these conditions, what becomes more important is learning from mistakes, not hiding or denying them. Children become less anxious or fearful about telling their parents when they have misbehaved or made a mistake. They are more open to constructive criticism and more willing to confide in their parents or ask for advice about dilemmas in their lives.

Children also respect their parents more when parents can apologize and admit mistakes. Parents have more influence when their children respect them. Having more influence can counterbalance peer pressure and rebelliousness in later years.

Children imitate what they see.

METHODS

CHAPTER 4

Encouraging Behavior Change

Key Ideas

- Young children are motivated by success.

- Positive reinforcement programs teach positive behavior in a pleasant, supportive way.

- Children should be rewarded for trying to reach a goal as well as for actually completing the goal.

- Rewards should include a lot of social reinforcement such as hugs, praise, and compliments.

- Shaping lasting positive behavior and values takes time and consistency.

Important Definitions

1. **Reward or positive reinforcement:** Something that is given or happens after a behavior that increases or strengthens the chance of that behavior happening again. Rewards and positive reinforcement are pleasurable or desirable and can be tangible, social, or symbolic, such as food, praise, or stickers. Positive reinforcement does not only refer to reinforcing positive behavior. Positive reinforcement can also work to reinforce misbehavior, such as when the whole class laughs at the disruptive antics of the class clown. Positive reinforcement refers to increasing a behavior, not the quality or goodness of that behavior.

2. **Bribe:** Bribes are payments for illegal or wrong behavior. Bribes are not the same as rewards. Rewards are given in return for or acknowledgment of good or praiseworthy behavior.

3. **Negative consequences:** Negative consequences are unpleasant results or actions that happen or are given after a behavior has occurred. Negative consequences decrease or weaken the chances of that behavior happening again.

Attention is a very powerful positive reinforcer.

How Behavior Is Learned

Goals for Children:

- Practice proper behavior
- Learn the benefits of behaving correctly and appropriately

Goals for Parents:

- Learn how to avoid "accidentally" rewarding misbehavior
- Learn how to shape your child's behavior constructively
- Learn how to set up a positive reinforcement program
- Learn to look for patterns to maintain or alter

Behavior is learned through a process of receiving rewards, or positive reinforcement, or through receiving punishments, or negative consequences, for conduct. Rewards and punishments ordinarily happen naturally, in an unplanned way. For example, peer attention can be a very strong positive reinforcer. When a class laughs at a child's misbehavior, that child will be more likely to misbehave again if she or he enjoyed the attention.

By understanding how to use rewards and negative consequences to reach your long-term goals, you can learn to counteract naturally occurring events that shape bad behavior. You can also use your knowledge of rewards and negative consequences to reinforce naturally occurring events that promote good behavior by adding rewards for good work or conduct in school.

Understanding the principles of behavior change helps parents shape both simple and complicated behaviors, from specific behaviors like whining or slamming doors to more complex behaviors such as cooperation, neatness, or self-care. When parents take time to plan how they might shape their child's behavior, they can better teach their child how to behave properly. For example, children learn to ask politely, when asking politely consistently enough gets them what they want. However, children learn to whine when whining gets them what they want.

A major challenge for parents is reducing misbehavior while encouraging and teaching appropriate behavior. The most efficient way of changing behavior is to use generous amounts of rewards or positive reinforcement with sparing amounts of negative consequences. Over time, the consistent use of this combination will help children develop self-control and high self-esteem. The focus stays on teaching the child what to do by helping the child practice the right behavior instead of the misbehavior. As a result, more of the parent-child interactions will be positive and friendly.

Rewards or Positive Reinforcement

Technically, a reward or positive reinforcement is something (an effect or result) that will increase or strengthen the likelihood of a behav-

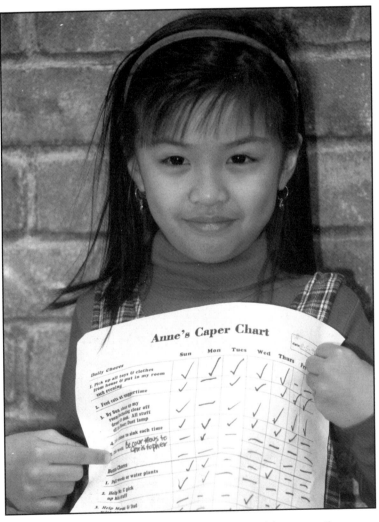

Positive reinforcement motivates children to change.

ior happening again. Rewards are desirable or pleasurable things that happen to someone after she or he has done something. Rewards are often mistakenly thought of as bribes. It is a mistake to view rewarding children as bribery because the aim of a bribe is to promote wrong or illegal behavior while the aim of a reward is to positively acknowledge good, appropriate behavior.

Rewards Help Children Get Started

Often, parents think rewards need to be material things, like toys or food, in order for children to feel motivated to try new behaviors. Sometimes parents think that rewards have to be expensive. However, rewards do not have to be big or expensive nor do rewards need to be only tangible or materialistic. Children are also motivated by choices and privileges, such as choosing what to eat, wear, or watch on TV, staying up later one night, or getting an extra story read to them at bedtime. Children will frequently work hard just for symbolic rewards like stickers, which, when accumulated, can be traded in for other types

Children are motivated by social rewards.

of rewards. They are very motivated by social rewards such as praise, hugs, and attention. Giving small rewards like stickers and praise often and immediately can be very powerful.

New behaviors that are encouraged through social rewards stick the longest, but tangible rewards may be needed at first to jump-start your child's motivation. You should always give tangible rewards with a great deal of praise and other social reinforcers. This pairing of tangible rewards with social rewards makes social rewards even more powerful and easier to use alone later. Combining social and material rewards will also reduce the chance that your child will only work for material rewards.

Once children have mastered the new behavior, they frequently tell their parents to quit giving them the material rewards because they have become proud of the accomplishment itself. This pride is what really makes the behavior "it's own reward." Normally, children like to master tasks and have no problem giving up the reinforcers that helped them achieve mastery. When this level is reached, getting rewards for the behavior often makes many children feel babyish and immature. A compliment from time to time is usually enough of a booster to keep children going in the desired direction.

Punishments or Negative Consequences

Negative consequences are punishments. However, most people think the word punishment means cruel or harsh. Experts therefore prefer the term *negative consequences*, which helps convey the message that although the consequences are undesirable, they are not intended to be harsh or mean. Technically, a negative consequence or punishment is any result or effect which will decrease or weaken the likelihood of a behavior happening again. Negative consequences are undesirable results that happen to someone after she or he has done something. Negative consequences are not punitive in nature, but are educational.

Teaching and Shaping Behavior

The most productive approaches to parenting emphasize methods that teach and strengthen desirable behavior while limiting and weakening undesirable behavior. You can promote more complex social behavior

such as cooperation, neatness, or self-care by setting up positive reinforcement programs.

Looking for patterns is the first step in understanding and changing
problem behaviors. A positive reinforcement program involves targeting
a specific positive behavior to increase. This target behavior is intended
to replace a negative behavior. Rewards are then used to increase this
selected behavior in a planned way. Rewards are given for behavior that
is close to the preferred behavior as well as for the preferred behavior
itself. For example, if the goal is to increase a child's ability to share, the
child is rewarded every time he or she shares without help from an
adult. Involving the child in planning the program, especially in choosing the rewards for the target behavior, is very important for success.

Attitudes Change After Behavior Changes

Sometimes, parents are opposed to giving praise or concrete rewards to children for doing routine family chores or responsibilities.

Children work hard for symbolic rewards.

Young children, however, are developmentally unable to fully understand why they need to do their fair share for the common good. Research shows that attitudes can change after behavior changes. So, by rewarding and praising your child for doing chores or following rules, you will help your child develop an understanding about the importance of being responsible and cooperative, because your child will experience the positive results of his or her effort. Maximizing the use of positive reinforcement makes family interactions more pleasant. Positive reinforcement will help your child feel more motivated to change. Children learn through success and family members feel better about each other.

Effective behavior-change programs build positive relationships between parents and children.

Basic Features of a Positive Reinforcement Program

Step 1: Start with one behavior at a time. Positive reinforcement programs begin with selecting one problematic behavior to change and determining what alternative behaviors, or *target behaviors*, are to be encouraged.

Step 2: Look for patterns. Next observe the occasions where behavior change is required. For three to seven days watch what ordinarily happens. Determine what might prompt and maintain the desirable target behavior and the undesirable behavior. Look for patterns in the way a situation develops. Consider what factors might be changed to help your child comply or perform the target behavior. Include a consideration of your own behavior that may unintentionally produce or reward the undesirable misbehavior.

Step 3: Break up the goal into smaller steps. Break the target behavior down into small, easily attainable steps that your child can understand. Tell your child the goal and why it is important. Tell your child that he or she will be rewarded for practicing the target behavior, that is, the behavior to be changed. Sometimes it is necessary to begin by rewarding behaviors that are similar to the final goal. Let your child have some input into what the rewards will be.

Step 4: Reward every time and as soon as possible. In the beginning, reward your child every time he or she produces the target behavior or its approximation. Reward as soon as possible. Small rewards given immediately are very powerful in initiating change. Always praise your child when he or she has performed the desired behavior or made efforts in the right direction.

Step 5: Use incentive systems. Incentive systems that involve tokens or symbols can be efficient and flexible. You can give your child small rewards, such as stickers or other tokens, every time he or she performs the target behavior. Your child can then cash in these tokens for larger rewards. For example, ten stickers earned for volunteering to help a sibling might allow your child to have a small toy or a privilege such as staying up fifteen minutes later one night. Remember, rewards do not need to be large or expensive.

Step 6: Strengthen the new behavior. Once the new behavior happens consistently, gradually increase what your child needs to do in order to get a reward. Once the new behavior is well established, continue to reward it, but not every time. This type of unpredictable or intermittent schedule of rewards greatly strengthens any behavior. Praise should still be given every time the desirable new behavior occurs. Over time, praise alone is usually sufficient to maintain the desirable behavior because your child will feel successful, and these feelings alone are powerful rewards.

Step 7: Reevaluate as needed. If a positive reinforcement program is not working, then consider the following:

- Are the rewards powerful enough?
- Are the steps toward the goal too big?
- Are other reinforcers in operation that are more powerful than the rewards offered by you? For example, peer attention may be the source of rewards that are actually reinforcing misbehavior.

Make Your Child a Partner in Change

When setting up a positive reinforcement system, making your child feel like a partner with you in learning and maintaining the desirable behavior is very important. Include your child in the discussion of what the program should be like. Older children can negotiate more of the specific features like the rewards, time frame for change, and how much change should be expected at each level.

Children are usually interested in getting the rewards and are motivated to start the program. Initially, however, some children may be reluctant. If this is the case for you, talk more with your child and try to discover what may be behind the reluctance. Sometimes children feel too anxious that they will fail or may be confused about what they need to do. They may actually feel insulted or embarrassed for needing such a program. You should reassure your child that the aim of the program is to learn a new habit and that if the program is not working, you will work together to figure out what needs to be changed to make the program more helpful.

CHAPTER 5

Building Cooperation

Key Ideas

- Self-control is a skill we learn; we are not born with it.

- Teaching is more effective than punishing.

- Children learn best when they are given choices and consequences that are clear and fit their age and abilities.

- When parents are consistent, they teach their children how to behave well and cooperate over time.

- Testing limits is normal and necessary for children to learn rules and develop self-control.

Important Definitions

1. **Structuring the environment:** Reducing a child's choices; giving a child specific rules, directions, and guidelines for a task.

> *You structure the environment all the time. For example, when you put a dessert out of sight so your child won't get into it before dinner, you have structured the environment. When you lock your home in the evening, you are structuring your environment.*

2. **Forced choices:** Giving the child a choice between two or more possibilities, which the parent has already picked out. Multiple-choice questions are forced choices.

   Hint: Offer only two choices whenever possible.

3. **Power struggle:** An expression that describes a situation where two people or groups in a conflict are unwilling to compromise.

4. **Consistency:** In parenting, consistency means that a parent behaves in a predictable, logical way so that a child knows what kinds of consequences to expect; a child predictably gets negative consequences for particular kinds of misbehaviors and rewards for particular positive behaviors and does not sometimes get rewarded and sometimes get punished for the same sort of thing. For example, if children sometimes get what they want and sometimes do not when they whine, this would be inconsistency in parenting. If children do not get what they want when they whine, but do get what they want when they behave properly, this would be consistency in parenting.

Learning to Cooperate Is Hard

Goals for Children:

- Learn consequences of behavior
- Stop acting on impulse
- Learn the benefits of cooperation

Goals for Parents:

- Learn to structure choices and consequences that fit the child's age and ability
- Set and enforce limits consistently
- Learn to develop and give consequences that are consistent and predictable

Children learn through experience that cooperation is advantageous.

Cooperation is difficult at any age. It is a hard skill to learn because the benefits of cooperation may not be experienced quickly. If a child takes turns, the child must wait and be without until his or her turn or a child must give up something before she or he is ready to do so. Children rarely respond immediately and with enthusiasm to a parent's instructions to do a chore or stop doing something fun. Learning to cooperate takes time.

Learning to behave cooperatively involves the following:

1. *Learning to control one's immediate urges and desires*—which means being able to delay or do without satisfaction.

2. *Being able to remember past consequences*—which depends on having predictable, consistent consequences.

3. *Being able to think ahead*—which requires a child to compare the current situation with past situations and consequences.

4. *Being able to care about the consequences*—which depends on having relationships that are positive enough to care about.

Choices and Consequences Help Children Learn

Parents sometimes move directly from making a request or a demand to scolding or spanking. However, when children do not immediately obey, they are not necessarily trying to be ornery, uncooperative, or defiant. Young children are still in the process of learning how to think over consequences, how to evaluate choices, and how to stop themselves from acting on impulse. Adding some extra teaching steps between parental demands and the delivery of negative consequences can help children learn to cooperate.

The best way to teach a child how to cooperate is to give choices and consequences to consider. These choices and consequences should be presented in a way that is easily understood by the child, who may be upset at the time. They should also fit the child's developmental abilities. Your child will learn better when you present the choices and consequences in a clear sequence of increasingly firmer choices and consequences. Putting choices in a sequence takes more time, but will give your child several opportunities to cooperate while making each step firmer and more restrictive. Presenting a series of choices and consequences maintains your authority while teaching your child how to cooperate.

Teaching Cooperation

In the following paragraphs, five levels of increasing parental control are described that can be used as steps in teaching cooperation. At each level the parent becomes firmer and more restrictive in response to a child's refusal or inability to cooperate. In real conflict situations, parents would not necessarily need to go through all five levels in the order presented here. Every situation is unique. You may need to skip a level or even go down to a less restrictive level depending on your child's response.

The Five Levels of Increasing Parental Control

Level 1: Preparing children

Level 2: Increasing structure and encouraging children

Level 3: Maintaining your own self-control

Level 4: Warning of impending consequences

Level 5: Setting limits and enforcing consequences

Level 1: Preparing Children
Method:

- Advance Notice

Young children, like adults, are frequently more cooperative when given advance notice of a required change in activity. Preparing children gives them the time and opportunity to shift from a preferred activity to one requested by the parent. Five minutes' advance notice is a good rule of thumb.

Examples of parent statements:

- "Three more jumps, then it's time to get out of the water."
- "In five minutes it will be time to wash your hands and come eat lunch."

Hint: When there's enough time, have your child repeat your instructions so you will both know she or he understood you. Ask in a friendly tone.

- "Now what did I say?"
- "Can you tell me what I just said?"

Hint: Compliment your child when she or he repeats accurately what you have said.

- "That's right! You sure are a good listener."
- "I sure do appreciate it when you listen to me."
- "Thank you for listening carefully."

Children frequently have more difficulty with self-control at important social functions or on outings such as trips to the grocery store. They can easily become excited or bored and start to misbehave. Advance preparation will help your child be more cooperative. Calmly instruct him or her beforehand on what is required for an upcoming situation. This not only reminds your child of the specific guidelines for behavior, but also gives your child time to adjust to your expectations. Preparing children also keeps the rules fresh in their memories, which makes following the rules less difficult. Advance preparation could include rehearsal of specific behaviors such as proper responses to greetings and verbal descriptions of rules.

Examples of parent statements with younger children:

- "We will be leaving for the grocery store in about five minutes. When we get there, I will let you pick out one special treat you want, but I do not want to hear you nag me for lots of other stuff. You can get one thing and that's all."
- "We will be going to a wedding this morning. Our good friends Jane and Richard are getting married. A wedding is a very special time. It is both happy and serious. When the wedding begins we must be very quiet so that everyone can pay attention and hear what is being said. Being quiet shows Jane and Richard that you like and respect them. You being still and quiet is a like a gift—a wedding present to them. It is very important. I will be with you the whole time. Can you try to be very quiet and still during the wedding? It will last about half an hour."
- "Now if other children try to get you to run around and bump into the dancers, you can say, 'No, I don't want to hurt anyone' or 'No, that would be rude.'"

Older children also benefit when parents provide advance cues that help them develop the ability to plan ahead. Parents help children learn to better organize their activities over longer time periods by reminding them of the time requirements for activities, what is needed, and other such helpful information. By doing this, parents provide children with a bridge while they are learning responsible planning and time management.

Examples of parent statements with elementary-age children:

- "Remember, your homework must be finished by seven o'clock or you will not be able to watch your favorite show."
- "That project of yours is due next week, right? Do you need to get anything from the store or the library in order to finish it on time? If you do, we need to get our schedules together because I'm really pressed for time this week."
- "If you want a clean uniform for the next game, it has to be in the clothes hamper by bedtime tonight."

Level 2: Increasing Structure and Encouraging Children

Methods:

- Structuring the environment by:
    - a. Using forced choices
    - b. Breaking up a chore into small tasks
- Giving positive instructions of what to do
- Using "please" and "thank you"
- Using empathy, humor, praise, and rewards

Structuring the environment

Level 2 responses involve encouraging children and increasing environmental structure. Here, you structure by giving specific guidelines and directions for tasks. For example, a parent might say, "Please put your dishes in the sink," rather than the less specific "Please clean up after yourself." Increasing structure by breaking up a chore into smaller tasks or using forced choices makes cooperating easier for children. Also, parents are structuring the environment when they plan ahead for outings or errands by bringing toys or items for the child that will keep the child's attention and prevent the child from misbehaving out of boredom.

Forced choices are several choices that have already been selected by the parent; the child must choose from these preselected choices. For example, the parent might say, "Do you want to put up your clothes first or your trucks?" Forced choices are helpful. They make choices simple and give children some measure of control over what they must do. Having some control, however small, can help children feel more cooperative. Breaking up a chore into smaller chunks of work makes a task less overwhelming. For example, instead of saying, "Go clean your room," a parent could say, "Start with putting your dirty clothes in the basket and then get your toys out of the living room, please."

Positive instructions

As much as possible, tell your child *what to do* rather than telling him or her what *not* to do. For example, parents frequently give commands in the negative such as, "Don't do that!" or "Stop running!" Children usually keep a better attitude when parents use a reminder of the proper behavior instead of a criticism of their current misbehavior. Also, young children may not be trying to misbehave. They just do not always remember in the heat of the moment the best or safest way to behave. Reminding them of what to do helps them remember and get back in control. With practice, you'll find that turning "don't do that" statements into positive instructions or directions is easier than you expected.

Negative Instructions	Positive Instructions
"Stop running."	"Walk or march."
"Don't get up there!"	"Stay here; be still."
"Don't be rude."	"Remember your manners."
"Quit whining."	"Use a regular voice."
"Quit yelling!"	"Use an inside (quiet) voice."
"Don't yell just because he yelled."	"Be a leader; be a good friend."
"Shut up."	"Please wait until I'm finished talking."

"Please" and "thank you"

Parents should model good manners by saying "please" and "thank you" when making any request of their child. Whenever possible parents should also use "please" as a first step with all mandatory directives or commands. Under these circumstances, the "please" does not mean that the parent is giving the child a choice over whether or not to follow the directive. The "please" here really means "please cooperate with my directive." Using "please" with a clear directive sets a positive tone and increases the likelihood that the child will cooperate. This, in turn, increases the likelihood that the child can be reinforced for collaboration and compliance. Parents can stop using "please" if the child does not obey after this initial request for cooperation. Otherwise, the child may become confused about what is expected of him or her (that is, what is truly optional and for how long).

Sometimes a child's immediate compliance is necessary for safety reasons or other important priorities, and parents must give commands without using "please." However, most situations allow a request for cooperation combined with the parental directive. Whenever possible, a *request* for cooperation should precede a *directive*, because this gives the child a cue or reminder of what is expected and an opportunity to comply. This intermediate step helps children learn how to judge choices and consequences. Parents can easily shift to making a demand with clearly defined limits and consequences if the child refuses to comply.

Using "please" also helps children learn how to make requests in a respectful manner. In adult work settings, supervisors get better results when they issue directives in a respectful manner. Children whose parents model courteous requests and directives are more likely to develop the positive social skills that promote success in adult life.

Examples of parent statements:

(A directive with a request for cooperation)

- "Please get your toys out of the kitchen."
- "Please keep your hands off the display table."

(A directive after the child has refused the request for cooperation)

- "I asked you once already to get your toys out of the kitchen. You need to get them out now."
- "It's not okay to pull the stuff off the store shelf. You need to keep your hands to yourself."

When your child complies with the request for cooperation, you can immediately reinforce cooperation by saying "thank you." Children should be thanked when they have obeyed even if the child has put up some resistance before finally complying with the parental demand. Thanking children not only models courtesy but also acknowledges that they have shown self-control and have done something they did not want to do. Children then feel appreciated and understood. The probability of future cooperative behavior increases.

Examples of parent statements:

- "Thank you for cooperating with me even though you didn't want to."
- "Thank you for taking your toys to your room. I really appreciate you doing what I asked you to do."

Empathy, humor, praise, and rewards

Positive techniques such as empathy, humor, praise, and rewards are very powerful. These methods tend to be underused because they require more effort and they may be seen as giving in or giving control

Children feel more cooperative when parents are polite and give positive instructions to them.

to the child. However, parents who use these positive techniques find that, over time, they can often prevent power struggles and bring a pleasant tone to interactions. These methods give children more opportunities to be cooperative and to be recognized in a positive way for their efforts. Then in the long run, parents spend less time stamping out negative behavior and more time engaged in positive exchanges.

Examples of parent statements:

Empathy: • "I know you want to keep on playing. I don't like to stop having fun either."
• "I know you don't like me to say, 'No.'"

Humor: (*Humor is not teasing a child or making fun of him or her. Humor means making a chore fun, being playful, or finding some way to make your child laugh with you.*)
• "I'm going to start your cleanup motor. I'm cranking your engine now! Crank, crank, crank!"
• "Let's pretend you're a bird and fly to dinner."

Praise: • "You sure are fast at this!"
• "You really know where things go!"
• "You're such a good helper!"

Reward: • "If you take your bath and brush your teeth without fussing, we will have time for an extra bedtime story."
• "You did such a good job, I think you deserve a special treat. How about making bedtime ten minutes later tonight?"

Level 3: Maintaining Your Own Self-Control

Methods:

• Taking a break if necessary
• Starting over and giving a warning of consequence for uncooperativeness

Level 3 responses involve parents maintaining self-control when provoked to anger by their child's defiance. Most young children, no matter how good natured they are, defy their parents at least occasionally if not frequently. This is an important and developmentally appropriate behavior. By testing rules or limits and having limits set and enforced, children develop a sense of identity and a set of expectations about the world. They learn social rules, consideration for others, and accountability—the fact that choices have consequences and individuals are responsible for their choices. However, parents often find challenges to their authority anger-provoking, draining, and sometimes hurtful. Maintaining self-control helps prevent the parent from making impulsive decisions and models appropriate expressions of anger for the child.

Parents can take a time-out themselves from a power struggle. This break is not a defeat or a setback. This time-out is an opportunity to show your child how to control anger when provoked. Cooling off and coming back to the situation in a more rational frame of mind is always helpful.

Examples of parent statements:

- "I'm getting very angry right now so I'm going to take a break for a minute and then we'll start again."

(When you return, state the action you want your child to take by a stated time limit. State the consequence that will happen if your child does not follow directive).

- "Okay, I'm calmer now. Here's the deal; you need to put your toys away by the time the timer goes off or I will put up your favorite toys for two days."

Level 4: Warning of Impending Negative Consequences for Misbehavior

Method:

- Warning

Level 4 responses involve warning children of the negative consequences that will occur if the misbehavior continues. Warning is a crucial but frequently omitted step in discipline. Parents often end up saying, "Okay, that's it! You can't . . . " without any real warning given. Warning children prompts them to recall and think about their past experiences with similar situations and negative consequences. This middle step between parental demands and punishments also provides the child another opportunity to practice good judgment and cooperate.

Examples of parent statements:

- "If you do not . . . (what you want your child to do), then . . . (state the consequence)."
- "If you do not <u>start picking up your room</u>, then I will <u>take away . . .</u> (a privilege or a toy)."
- If you do not <u>get back in control</u>, you will need to <u>go to time-out until you are in control.</u>"

Warning children gives them another chance to cooperate.

Level 5: Setting and Enforcing Limits

Methods:

- Setting limits
- Enforcing limits with negative consequences

Level 5 involves setting limits and enforcing them with negative consequences. When parents do this consistently, their children learn that cooperating prevents undesirable outcomes. Children are then more likely to be cooperative because they know from past experience that their parents will follow through with undesirable consequences for misbehavior. Parents should state the rule that was broken or the infraction made by the child. Then follow through on the consequence given in the warning.

*Setting and enforcing limits consistently
helps children learn to cooperate.*

Examples of parent statements:

- "I told you that if you did not get back in control, you would need to go to time-out. You are not in control and now you need to go to time-out to get back in control."
- "I told you that if you left the yard again without permission you would have to stay in your room for the rest of the afternoon. You left without permission and now you need to go to your room."
- "I told you that you could not play with Daddy's things. You got into his stuff without permission and now you have lost the privilege of having a friend over today."

How many chances?

Young children frequently need several opportunities to make the right choice. After children show they have learned and can make the right choice promptly, parents can cut back on the number of steps or opportunities for choices they give a child. Children need much more guidance and direction from adults for a longer period of time than parents usually expect.

Self-Control Is a Skill We Learn

Most children do not want to misbehave, but they find not giving in to their urges very difficult. Even adults have difficulty denying their urges at times. We are not born with self-control. It is a skill we learn. Self-control takes a lot of practice. We find out through experience that self-control pays off in the long run and that defiance does not.

When you are consistent, you encourage cooperation and teach self-control because over time your child learns what to expect with misbehavior and what to expect with cooperation. Think of each situation as an opportunity to teach something that may sink in after many, many teaching sessions. Think of each incident as a step toward a long-range goal and not the deciding battle that must be won to save your child.

Parents are understandably frustrated when their children do not quickly and consistently do what they ask them to do. However, parents are not usually frustrated because the child is in danger of harm or harming someone else. They are most often frustrated because the mis-behavior is inconvenient or distressing for them. If a situation is not life threatening or potentially disastrous, take time to teach self-control rather than compliance. In the long run, children are better served when they learn how to control their impulses and understand the reasons why self-control is a valuable skill.

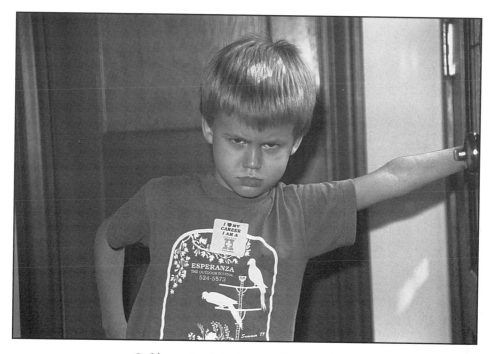

Self-control is learned over time.

CHAPTER 6

Negative Consequences

Key Ideas

- Parents teach self-control when they show self-control in disciplining.

- Negative consequences should be in proportion to the misbehavior and age of the child.

- When parents use aggressive disciplinary methods, they teach children to behave aggressively.

- Time-out works because it takes away reinforcement for misbehavior in a nonaggressive way.

- Teach children what to do by using penalties and practicing the correct behavior (behavioral rehearsal).

Important Definitions

1. **Intermittent reinforcement:** Intermittent reinforcement means that sometimes a behavior is rewarded, but sometimes it is not (rewards are given unpredictably or inconsistently). This is a very powerful type of reinforcement. Behavior shaped through intermittent reinforcement is very hard to change because reinforcement happens randomly. When a whining child sometimes gets what he or she wants by whining and sometimes does not, this is an example of intermittent reinforcement.

2. **Response cost or penalty system:** Although not a widely used term, response cost simply means to take away reinforcers such as toys or privileges if a child misbehaves. Response cost is used to decrease unwanted behavior.

> *You have probably used response cost already. If you have taken away a toy after your child has hit someone with it or refused to let your child watch TV after doing something wrong, then you have used response cost as part of your disciplinary methods. For a specific problem behavior that the child repeats over and over again, a combination of response cost along with a great deal of praise and positive reinforcement for the right behavior is more effective than response cost used alone.*

3. **Behavioral rehearsal:** Behavioral rehearsal involves practicing the correct behavior. When used as a negative consequence following a misbehavior, the child is required to repeat the correct behavior over and over again. This repetition helps the child practice the correct behavior so he or she can learn what to do. For example, if a child

slams a door, the child may be required to practice closing the door quietly from three to twenty times. (**Do less when children are younger or the misbehavior is not frequent; do more when children are older or the misbehavior is frequent**). This is a useful method for toddlers because their misbehavior is due more to not knowing the correct behavior or not having had enough practice doing the correct behaviors.

Practicing the correct behavior helps children learn what to do.

Aggressive Punishments are Counterproductive

Goals for Children:

- Learn to control impulses
- Learn to get back in control
- Learn appropriate and acceptable behaviors to do when angered

Goals for Parents:

- Use self-control to teach self-control
- Respect the child while respecting yourself
- Show constructive ways of responding to frustration

Because of their young age and developmental level and because they are still learning about the world, children often feel disappointment

Follow corrections with lots of support
and attention for good behavior.

and hurt more deeply than adults do. Try hard to remember this fact when disciplining your child. A scolding or punishment that seems mild to adults seems much harsher to children. If children feel their parents' anger and irritation more than their parents' love, they can begin to feel bad about themselves and their families. Follow up punishments or corrections with lots of support, hugs, and positive attention for good behavior.

Both children and adults feel criticisms more strongly than compliments. Too much criticism, regardless of the amount of positive interactions, can damage a child's self-esteem. A good rule of thumb is *Balance every negative interaction* (scolding, reprimand, negative consequence, and so on) *with many, many positive interactions* (hugs, positive attention, "I love you," and so on).

Inadvertently Increasing Misbehavior

Research studies consistently show that aggressive punishments such as spanking, shaming, and scolding actually increase misbehavior and decrease a child's moral growth, self-control, and self-esteem. Studies also

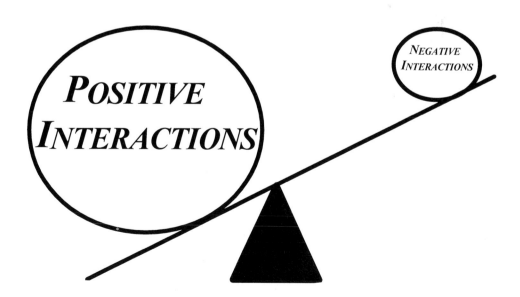

Balance every negative interaction with many,
many positive interactions.

show that children whose parents mainly use these disciplinary methods are much more likely to grow up feeling deeply depressed and become very aggressive, resentful, and angry.

Why would aggressive punishments increase misbehavior? Since the 1950s, much has been learned about human behavior. Aggression has been studied extensively in animals and humans. Now, most experts agree that when people are frightened, angered, or thwarted, they feel frustrated. When people or animals feel frustrated, their survival instinct can be aroused and displayed as aggressive behavior.

Children feel aggressive after they have been spanked because spanking angers and frustrates them. More importantly though, *children imitate what they see.* When parents are aggressive with their children, children imitate their parents and use aggressive behavior when they are angry or frustrated. They may learn that "might makes right" and use aggression to get what they want.

Many parents see no harm in an occasional mild swat on the bottom. Many parents say, "I was spanked and I'm okay," or "What's wrong with a little spanking now and then?" In truth, many children who have been spanked occasionally are okay, but that does not mean that spanking is a helpful disciplinary technique. Those children may be okay *despite* the spanking not because of it.

Parents usually spank when they are frustrated and feel that no other options are available. Most parents would not choose to spank their child if they were confident that other methods actually worked. Little support exists for parents to use methods that may take longer, but work better. Well-meaning friends or family members may say, "Just give a swat to show who's boss." However, teaching adaptive, appropriate, capable behavior takes more than simply reacting physically to the emotionally provoking behavior of our children. This teaching requires self-discipline from parents. Parents must contain their natural, normal impulses for the long-term best interest of the child and the family. Parents need support from others when they want to use nonaggressive methods.

Defiant Behaviors Are Provocative

When faced with aggressive and defiant behaviors, parents can understandably be provoked into scolding, shaming, nagging, or spanking children. Parents say, "But when I spank them, they stop." Scolding, shaming, nagging, or spanking often *does* work to interrupt the misbehavior promptly, but research shows that these methods do not help children learn self-control. In the long run, aggressive punishments are counterproductive. Aggressive punishments may lead children to be sneaky and repeat the misbehavior when the parent is not around to see it; they may not learn how to stop their impulses by themselves. Children may come to depend excessively on others or the environment to keep themselves in line. Children need to learn to control their impulses even when an authority is not around to enforce rules. A teaching approach to childhood misbehavior that emphasizes empathic, nonaggressive methods of discipline helps children develop an internal sense of right and wrong and personal direction.

Three Basic Reasons Why Scolding, Shaming, Nagging, and Spanking Are Not Effective Means of Disciplining Children

Reason 1: These types of aggressive punishments can actually teach children to behave aggressively because children copy what they see others do. Children can learn to use whining, complaining (a type of scolding), and even physical force to get what they want and not learn better ways of working out conflicts. For example, when a parent spanks a child, the child can come to believe that when people do not do what you want them to do, hitting them is okay.

Reason 2: Children take these episodes harder than adults and these bad feelings can ruin the child's relationship with the parent. Children often end up feeling resentful, shamed, and bad about themselves. As a result they are usually less interested in cooperating. They can become more interested in not getting caught the next time instead of learning how to behave properly. They can even become afraid of or anxious about being with their parents.

Reason 3: Parents are usually very angry when they nag, scold, or spank. The high emotion distracts parents and children from the real task, which is to teach children the right way to behave. Parents are distracted because they feel more like punishing or getting even than teaching. Children are distracted because they become afraid or anxious when their parents are so angry. A parent is not likely to have the same amount of emotion each time the same misbehavior happens and this makes it hard to be consistent. Sometimes the parent may give a strong punishment and sometimes the parent may simply be too worn-out to give a punishment or follow through on a punishment. If a parent is inconsistent in giving negative consequences, then the misbehavior can actually increase and become stronger. Gambling games like slot machines and video games work on an "intermittent reinforcement" system. With a slot machine, you might win any time you put in your money, even if you have just won. Because you never know when the next payoff is, a powerful incentive exists to keep putting in money. When we use intermittent reinforcement with children, they never know when a misbehavior will pay off. Consequently, children keep trying to win with these misbehaviors.

Be Matter-of-Fact

With good reason, parents are usually irritated or angry when it is time to give a negative consequence. Even though children need to understand that a parent is genuinely upset with them, parents should temper their emotional expression when delivering the negative consequence. Try to be as matter-of-fact as possible. To be effective, negative consequences should:

- Fit the child's developmental level
- Be in proportion to the misbehavior
- Fit the crime and be delivered in a timely fashion, not too long after the misbehavior has occurred but not before enough information about the misbehavior is known

As with rewards, the power of negative consequences that are too delayed will be diluted because of the time lag. The older the child, the longer the delay can be without losing its effectiveness. You should experiment to discover what works well for your own child. When parents deliver a negative consequence before gathering enough information about the situation, they may not be as effective in selecting what consequence to give and which child or children should receive a negative consequence. For example, was the misbehavior an accident or a true misbehavior? Is the child acting up because of feeling sick or tired? Was the child set up by friends or siblings?

Negative consequences should not be administered in a manner that is hostile, spiteful, or belittling to the child. Avoid sarcasm. Once the matter is settled, parents should calmly discuss the situation with the child. Show affection and tell the child the appropriate behaviors to use the next time.

Negative Consequences

- Time-out
- Time-out with physical holding
- Fines or penalties (response cost)
- Behavioral rehearsal (of appropriate behavior)

Time-Out

Time-out is a useful method for stopping aggressive and other undesirable behaviors. It signals to the child that the behavior is unacceptable and gives the child an opportunity to regain emotional control. Defiance often provokes anger in parents. When parents use time-out, they model nonaggressive and constructive responses to conflict for their child. Using time-out also models self-control in spite of angry feelings. Self-control is what children need to learn. Defiant behavior is primarily reinforced by basic social factors such as winning a power struggle or receiving attention from peers or parents. Time-out involves removing the child from immediate sources of reinforcement for undesirable behavior.

In practice, time-out from reinforcement means putting the child in a place that is safe and nonthreatening but is also unstimulating and away from sources of entertainment. **Avoid frightening places such as closets, attics, basements, or dark rooms.** For example, a chair or a corner can be used for time-out with preschool- and elementary-age children. Toddlers can be put in their playpen or crib.

Some parents object to using a crib as a time-out place because they are concerned that their children may form negative feelings about their crib and may then have problems sleeping. Whether or not a crib is used is not the important point. What is important is that time-out with toddlers can be effective as long as they can be confined safely. However, when toddlers protest going into their cribs, their protest is most likely because of their normal resistance to separation from their parents. It would be highly unlikely for toddlers to form negative feelings about their cribs from using them as a time-out place, because time-out with toddlers should be very infrequent. Infrequent use should not produce negative feelings from time-out alone. Time-out for toddlers should be restricted to very aggressive behaviors such as biting and hitting. For other typical problems, such as refusing to share or shift to another activity, toddlers can frequently be distracted or redirected. Also, toddlers are still usually small enough for parents to simply pick them up and move them when necessary and interest them in a new activity.

Time-out helps children practice self-control.

Although experts may differ on specific steps for time-out, the basic guidelines for time-out are as follows:

Step 1: Instruct the child about the rules for time-out and what time-out means. For example, a parent could say, "When you lose control and do things that hurt, you will go to time-out so you can get back in control."

Step 2: Establish the rules and practice time-out with your child before you use it. Practicing ahead of time is useful for two reasons. First, knowing what to expect helps children maintain self-control. Second, introducing new methods when people are upset is difficult.

Step 3: When time-out is necessary, parents should, in a firm voice, do the following:

- Point out to children what misbehavior has led to time-out.
- Tell them to go to time-out and remind them of the rules for time-out.
- Escort children to the time-out location if need be.

Step 4: Let children know what they must do to get out of time-out. For example, say, "To get out of time-out, you need to be quiet by the time the bell goes off."

Step 5: Speak in a calm but firm voice throughout the procedure and make empathic statements. For example, say, "I know you're angry with me, but the rule is no biting or hitting."

Step 6: The recommended time frame is one minute per year of a child's age up to ten minutes maximum. The length of time spent in time-out is not the key ingredient. Remember that the power of time-out comes from removing the child from the primary social reinforcers of defiant behaviors, such as attention. Using a timer with a bell where the child can hear it can help the child get back in control.

Step 7: If a child leaves time-out without permission or is otherwise not showing self-control, reset the timer for one additional minute. Repeat the rule about what the child needs to do in order to get out of time-out. Repeat this process as necessary until the child shows self-control by complying with time-out rules.

Refusal to Stay in Time-Out

Spanking children if they refuse to stay in time-out is not a good idea, nor is it necessary. When a child is spanked for not staying in time-out, the whole purpose of time-out is defeated. Time-out is a place for children to get back in control without reinforcement or attention for misbehavior. Spanking is negative attention for misbehavior and may reinforce the misbehavior as well as create the other problems associated with spanking as discussed earlier.

In addition, when children are spanked for refusing to stay in time-out, the goal changes. The purpose becomes having the child do time in time-out rather than the original goal of helping the child learn self-control and how to calm down. If time-out is not working, you should experiment with other types of consequences for misbehavior. There is nothing magical about time-out. Time-out is just one of many techniques available to parents to teach their children self-control and good manners.

For older children who continue to leave time-out or when time-out does not seem to help change misbehavior, parents should consider taking away privileges or using a targeted positive reinforcement program. For young children who are not physically strong enough to break loose from a parent, physical holding may be used sparingly after parents have received training in this technique from a qualified professional.

Time-Out with Physical Holding

For very young children, older toddlers and preschoolers, physical holding can be used when a child continues to leave time-out without permission and cannot be contained by any of the procedures suggested to this point. More importantly, however, physical holding can be used when children are so aggressive that injury to themselves or others or property damage is likely. Physical holding can keep the child and parent safe while maintaining the parent's authority. Children who are this aggressive may be feeling very upset about something they cannot put into words. Consulting a professional for an evaluation to better determine what might be behind such intense emotions is highly recommended. Especially with children, prevention and early intervention are invaluable.

You should not attempt physical holding without consultation and direction from a qualified professional since accidental injury could occur to either parent or child. The technique is described so that parents will know about this alternative disciplinary method. *To find a qualified professional, call your local psychological, psychiatric, or social work associations; United Way Information and Referral Service; public school district; local, county, or state public mental health authority; or consult your family physician.*

When you first use physical holding, your child may protest that he or she is being hurt. These complaints should be taken seriously. Use common sense to judge whether or not you are holding in a hurtful way. Not much effort is required to hold a normal child having a tantrum, but proper technique is crucial.

Under ordinary circumstances, the technique of physical holding should help children regain emotional control within a brief period of time. Normally, physical holding should not exceed ten to fifteen minutes. A child would rarely, if ever, need this level of restraint. If physical restraint is necessary on more than two or three occasions, an evaluation by a professional would be helpful for both parent and child.

After your child is calm, you should both discuss what led up to time-out and the physical holding, and investigate alternative behaviors that could be used to maintain self-control in the future. Be sure to show acceptance and affection for your child.

Procedure

Step 1: Begin the procedure for physical holding by reminding the child that he or she needs to get back in control and stay in time-out. Move in close to the child and provide the minimum physical touching needed to keep the child in time-out. If greater restraint is necessary, hold the child in your lap. If necessary, position your back against the wall for support.

Step 2: Hold the child's wrists and cross the child's arms over his or her chest. Cross your legs over the child's legs. This is called a *basket hold* because you are cradling your child as if he or she is inside a basket. Holding the child firmly, but not too tightly, prevents the child from twisting and hitting, which can hurt both child and parent.

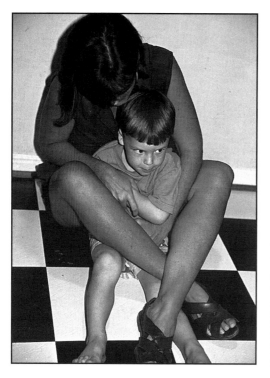 

Training in physical holding from a qualified professional
is necessary to prevent injury to both parent and child.

Step 3: Making empathic statements whenever possible will help both parent and child calm down. For example, "I know you're upset, but it's not okay to hit." Let the child know what he or she must do to be released. "You need to calm down and then I'll let you go." When the child is calm, give the child an illusion of choice by asking the child which arm should be released first. Release arms and legs one at a time to show your child you are still in control of the situation. At this point, you should be in a hugging position.

Step 4: Talk to your child about what led up to physical holding. Be supportive and forgiving, not preachy and angry. Parents have the option of letting their child leave time-out after this discussion or making their child finish the rest of time-out in a calm manner. You should use your own discretion when making this choice. Factors to consider are your child's temperament and the purpose of time-out, which is, in essence, an opportunity for children to regain emotional control.

Show affection and be forgiving.

Most often defiant behavior does not involve direct, physical aggression by the child. Defiance usually takes more passive forms of resistance such as refusal, dawdling, whining, and fussing. While these behaviors are certainly provocative and frustrating, save time-out for excessively aggressive behaviors rather than plain old stubbornness or uncooperativeness. The overuse of time-out diminishes its power. Also, time-out is not effective or practical in all situations.

Alternative methods for handling disobedience or misbehavior exist. You can penalize or fine your child to decrease or weaken undesirable behavior. You can also rehearse appropriate behavior as a means of correcting infractions.

Response Cost

Using a penalty or fine to reduce child misbehavior involves taking away privileges or toys for a brief period of time. Children should be informed of specific penalty policies before using this strategy in order to shape accurate expectations and to avoid the buildup of resentment. Penalties are surprisingly effective, especially when given in the context of a warning about what will happen if the child continues misbehaving.

Example situation: Child repeatedly breaks a rule.

Basic setup: Describe what rule was broken and why the rule is important. State what the negative consequence will be for forgetting the rule the next time. Have the child repeat the rule and consequence of forgetting.

- "You know, I have had to tell you many, many times not to leave the yard without permission. I need to know where you are all the time. That's the only way I can do my job and make sure you are safe. You seem to need some help being able to remember the rule about asking first before you leave the yard. So, to help you learn to remember that rule, the next time you leave the yard without permission, I'm going to take away your trucks for two days."

Have your child repeat what the rule is that was forgotten and what will happen the next time the rule is forgotten. Expect your child to promptly forget the rule and require you to enforce the consequence. Remember that while this testing of the limits by your child is irritating to you, it will turn out to be a helpful experience for your child as long as you enforce the consequence. Children need to experience limits, whether they agree with them or not, and learn accountability and appropriate behaviors. One way they learn is to break the rule and experience the consequences.

Example of response cost in the context of a warning:

- "If you two keep bickering, neither of you will get to watch TV when we get home. If you can't say something nice, then don't say anything at all."

Behavioral Rehearsal (of Appropriate Behavior)

Another response to misbehavior requires the child to rehearse an appropriate alternative behavior. Again, the emphasis is on teaching the child what to do instead of the misbehavior. Behavioral rehearsal involves having the child correct an infraction as soon as possible by repeating or practicing the proper behavior over and over again. Parents should explain why the alternative behavior is better. This method teaches children, in a positive fashion, how to perform the desired behavior. It is a useful method for toddlers who misbehave mostly because they don't know any better or haven't had enough practice with the correct behaviors. The general rule of thumb is to require less repetitions when children are younger or when the misbehavior is not frequent; and require more repetitions when children are older, or when the misbehavior is frequent.

For example, when children slam a door, have them open and close the door gently many times to practice the proper door-shutting behavior. For younger children who do not have much language ability yet, parents can physically rehearse the event with them by gently guiding the child through the proper behavioral sequence. Toddlers frequently find this to be as much fun as the inappropriate behavior was and a power struggle may be avoided.

Having a child make amends for hurting another child by practicing proper behavior can also teach self-control. An example in the case of hitting or biting would be to make the child kiss or stroke softly the hurt area while saying "I'm sorry." Children who cannot yet talk can also be guided through this sequence. The parent physically guides the child through the motions while saying "I'm sorry" for the child. Speaking for the child and physically guiding in this way models the right thing to do.

Examples of parent statements and actions:

- "It's not okay to slam doors. Slamming the door could break it and it makes too much noise. It hurts my ears. I want you to practice shutting the door gently three times. Okay, let's start . . ." (*After the child is finished*) "Great! I hope next time you'll remember to shut the door gently."
- (*While parent helps the child gently stroke the pet*) "Let's use soft touches on kitty. Soft, soft."

Behavioral rehearsal teaches children what to do.

COMMON MISBEHAVIORS

CHAPTER 7

Toddlers

(approximately twelve months to three years)

Key Ideas

- The main psychological tasks for toddlers are to learn they are unique individuals and to develop a sense of competence.

- Toddlers learn they are distinct, unique individuals by exploring their environment and practicing separateness, competency, and independence from others.

- The negativism of toddlers is not true defiance. Negativism is a combination of normal immaturity and the way toddlers experience their separateness.

- Parents who use methods that combine encouragement, instruction, and calm discipline can promote competence and self-esteem while preventing the development of serious problems.

Important Definitions

1. **Autonomy:** In child development, autonomy means having the ability to do life's tasks on one's own. Children have a natural urge to develop and learn how to take care of themselves. As they mature, they become increasingly self-sufficient or autonomous.

2. **Rapprochement:** (pronounced: rah-prosh-mont) Rapprochement comes from the French word *rapprocher,* which means to bring together or reconcile. In child development, rapprochement refers to the developmental phase in which toddlers begin to establish their independence. Toddlers gradually alternate between exploring their environment apart from their parents and seeking comfort or security by being physically close to their parents. In this phase, toddlers will run off from their parents and expect their parents to run after them. On other occasions, they will play contentedly as long as the parents are physically present and attending to them or they will cling desperately to parents and not let them out of their sight. This phase is so universal that child development professionals believe that rapprochement is a necessary developmental stage where children learn to practice independence safely.

3. **Separation Protest:** At about seven to twelve months of age, children begin to cry when their parents leave them (separation protest). As a rule, children are easily soothed. However, as toddlers develop a strong sense of their separate identity, this crying can become very intense even when they are left with familiar caregivers and even if they have not previously protested separation. This is because toddlers realize, as seperate individuals, they are vulnerable and begin to fear abandonment by their parents. Toddlers usually calm down quickly after the parent has left. However, it is not unusual for toddlers to go through periods when they are not easily soothed. This more intense period of separation protest can start as early as fourteen months and ordinarily subsides by two years of age.

Children naturally want to learn how to take care of themselves.

Overview of the Toddler Stage

Toddlers are "here and now; out of sight, out of mind" people. Exploring the environment through action and direct experience is a toddler's most important way of learning. Repetition, a key characteristic of this age, is critical to helping toddlers develop their memories and their ability to understand and master their environment. They want the same story read over and over, the same game played over and over. Because of their short memories and attention spans, toddlers are easily redirected to new activities.

As toddlers mature and approach preschool age, they are able to understand simple cause-and-effect relationships such as anticipating what will happen next in a game and following simple directions. Also, as their memories improve, toddlers are more persistent about going after what they want. When they are about two and a half years old, toddlers are in a transitional period and begin to show some characteristics of preschoolers.

Toddlers are driven to figure out what they can do.

Toddlers are naturally and powerfully driven to figure out who they are (identity and separateness) and what they can do (self-sufficiency and competence). Toddlers, even older toddlers, are impulsive, with little or no ability to think ahead about the consequences of their actions. They also have very limited language and physical skills. The internal drive to explore and develop themselves combined with limited skills and abilities often frustrates toddlers so much that they fall apart emotionally. Toddlers usually express frustration immediately, intensely, and at a high volume.

To master their environment, toddlers must expand their ability to delay satisfaction or gratification. Language skills and the ability to remember are crucial to tolerating this delay. As a child's language skills grow, the child can recall objects not physically present. Being able to recall events and objects helps the toddler learn from experiences with consequences. When a child has these capacities, words become more meaningful because the child can connect them to experiences and remember the connection. The parent can say, "If you do *this* now, you will get *that* later," and the child can picture what is being traded and consider if the trade is worth the wait.

Key Developmental Themes: Separation and Individuation

During infancy, all of a child's needs must be taken care of by parents and other caretakers. Babies have no concept that they are separate individuals. As babies develop psychologically, they begin to understand that they are separate and capable of doing things independently. Resistance to what others want them to do is one important way toddlers learn and express this increasingly independent control over their minds and bodies. This resistance is often referred to as negativism, striving for autonomy, or, in exasperation, the Terrible Twos.

Toddlers also develop a sense of separate identity and independence by learning to cope with brief periods of separation from their parents. As they begin to form their separate identity, they begin to fear being abandoned by their parents. During the rapprochement phase, toddlers go through a period called *separation protest*, when they will cry and protest out of fear or anxiety about being left with someone other than a parent, even familiar caregivers.

Separation protest can upset parents because the child's emotional reactions are usually very intense. However, children who are in good hands when parents leave learn that parents return predictably and reliably. The separation and reunion process helps children practice independence and learn how to cope with life. Children develop a deep trust

*Separations that are followed by reliable
reunions promote independence.*

that their parents love them even when not in their physical presence. The experience of anxiety, separation, and coping followed by a reliable reunion with parents assists children in their overall development.

Parents want their children to become increasingly independent and self-sufficient. However, they must endure more frequent clashes as this self-sufficiency evolves. This process can be draining and stressful for parents. When toddlers express resistance and defiance, they are not being disrespectful or rebellious in the usual sense of these words. They do not have a concept of disrespect or rebellion. Toddlers are at work developing their concept of themselves as separate individuals. Resistance to parental demands is the way toddlers make clear to themselves that they are distinct individuals. When parents remember that this stage of refusal and defiance is universal and psychologically essential, they can better prepare for managing these situations to assist their child's overall development.

Reducing excessive frustration helps toddlers
focus on mastering their environment.

Implications for Discipline

Most misbehavior in this age range comes from toddlers having little or no capacity to delay their impulses. Focus mostly on providing opportunities to explore safely and redirecting your toddler's interests when necessary. This will provide a stimulating and empathic environment. This environment best promotes a child's development of competence and independence.

Parents of toddlers can set the foundations for the long-term guidance of their children by using the basic principles and methods described in this book. Maintaining an empathic style while setting limits fosters the closeness necessary for a child to feel valued and motivated to cooperate. Parents who can help their toddlers practice and tolerate delay help them learn that self-control over their impulses is expected and necessary. Parents who can structure the environment to reduce excessive amounts of frustration help their children focus on mastering the environment instead of feeling defeated by it. This helps them adjust more easily to disappointments and limit-setting because they develop expectations that patience and effort will lead to positive outcomes more often than the negative ones.

Remember that toddlers are too young to understand fully the consequences of their actions. This ability to learn the connection between behaviors and consequences has its roots in the exploration characteristic of this stage. The ability to make this connection does not become sufficiently developed for self-control until children have more memory and complex language skills, which evolve throughout childhood and adolescence.

Even though toddlers have limited language skills, parents should continue to talk to them. While they do not understand the words, they do understand the tone and the overall message about their behavior and the parent-child relationship. Also, using language at this age sets the stage for later ages when language skills are well developed and discussing problems is necessary. Toddlers cannot respond to reason or logic, but parents can still introduce in simple words basic rationales and explanations for certain limits and standards of conduct. With repetition, toddlers begin to expect that they are required to follow these rules and standards. Toddlers carry over these expectations into the next stage.

Common Misbehaviors

- Running off from parents
- Temper tantrums
- Difficulty sharing possessions

Running off from Parents

Toddlers run off from parents frequently when they are in the rapprochement phase. This running off and looking expectantly for the parent to chase and catch them is one way toddlers practice being separate then being together again. This pattern helps them practice independence safely by providing a brief period of separation followed quickly by a reunion with the parent. Sometimes this pattern can be enjoyable for both parent and child. Playing the game of chase and catch, for instance, gives the toddler many opportunities to practice

A good harness keeps a child safe but allows exploration.

separation and reunion and may reduce the frequency of this behavior at other times.

When circumstances make this behavior unsafe or it repeatedly interferes with getting important tasks accomplished, parents can use a safety harness. A good quality harness that fits over the child's chest allows a toddler some freedom to explore safely but keeps the child within close supervision of the parent.

Some parents feel that a harness is demeaning to children. However, many toddlers enjoy the harness because it lets them have more freedom. Young toddlers are unaware of the harness itself. They are only aware that they cannot always do what they want to do. Some older toddlers even enjoy pretending they are a horse pulling a carriage or other such play. Older toddlers who have enough language to verbally protest being in a harness are usually old enough to understand the parent's expectations about safe and proper behavior outside of the home. These older toddlers can be instructed ahead of time about what behavior is expected of them and what consequence they will receive if they forget the rules.

Example of parent statement:

- "Today, we need to go to the mall for a while. If you don't want to wear the harness this time, you need to stay with me all the time. I will take the harness with me and if you run off, you will need to put the harness on. If you can remember the rule about staying with me, when we get home, I'll play a game with you."

Temper Tantrums

Toddlers usually throw temper tantrums when they are frustrated beyond their emotional capacity to tolerate such intense disappointment. They are not psychologically sophisticated enough to throw a temper tantrum in an attempt to manipulate an adult into giving them what they want. Soothing your toddler with empathic statements, hugs, and gentle restraint resolves many toddler temper tantrums. Toddlers respond well to empathic statements even when their language skills are just beginning. They respond not so much to the words but to the soothing tone. Using empathic words also helps you practice these kinds of statements. Therefore, when the child does have a better grasp of language you will already be accustomed to making empathic statements.

If your child is small enough, and leaving the situation is at all possible, you can simply pick up your toddler and leave while saying soothing, but firm statements. If he or she is throwing a tantrum over being confined (such as in a carseat), you can help your child calm down by making empathic statements and making efforts to redirect your child's interest. Young toddlers can often be interested in a toy or some new activity like singing songs or a naming game. Their memories are not well developed and they quickly forget about what initially prompted their tantrum. Remaining calm during a tantrum is helpful; strongly expressed negative emotion from the parent accelerates the

Removing a toddler from a frustrating situation
can help calm and redirect the child.

tantrum and it models negative emotional expression in response to frustration.

Examples of parent statements:

- "I know you're upset. We'll be home soon. What's that animal called on the sign over there?"
- "I know you don't like that carseat. Let's sing some songs."
- "I know you're upset. It's hard to stop playing with the ball. How about playing with this dinosaur?"
- "Are you having trouble getting that toy to fit? May I help you?" (*If your child consents*) "Try it this way, honey." (*If your child does not want your help*) "Okay, I can see you want to do it yourself, that's good you want to do it yourself. Let me know if you want help."

If leaving the situation entirely is not possible, taking your child to a more private location can help him or her to calm down. Going outside or to a restroom or another more private location will allow you and your child to handle the situation with more privacy and less distraction. Younger toddlers may quickly calm down when presented with an acceptable alternative; older toddlers may respond to either redirecting or the chance to earn something they want later in exchange for calm behavior in the present. When toddlers are close to three years of age and have better memories and vocabularies, they may be able to respond well to earning something later for calming down now. Try this option from time to time as toddlers grow older, because they are in a transition and their ability to use this type of reasoning may grow rapidly and unexpectedly.

Examples of parent statements:

- "I know you wanted that toy, but I am not going to get it for you."
- "I know you're disappointed I won't get you that candy bar."
- "You need to stay with me. It's not okay to run all over the store."
- "It's upsetting when we don't get what we want, but we have to learn how to deal with not getting what we want lots of times."

- "If you can calm down, we'll go back and look at all the fish swimming around in their tank before we leave. Would you like to see the fish again?"

Difficulty Sharing Possessions

Toddlers can be fickle about sharing. Sometimes they are generous to a fault, but mostly they are quite unwilling to share. "Mine" is a frequently heard word from toddlers about their possessions and all objects they want to possess. If they want it, they think it belongs to them. Toddlers in day care have experiences daily with sharing and taking turns under adult guidance, yet they still can find sharing difficult.

Try not to make your toddler feel guilty about his or her unwillingness to share. Part of learning about separateness involves an intense

Sharing is often difficult for toddlers.

focus on needs, wants, and the control over personal possessions. Toddlers don't realize that sharing doesn't result in losing their toys permanently. They are inexperienced with the benefits of sharing, which become clearer to them when they are older and can enjoy playing with peers.

You can help your toddler by making some toys shareable and others not. When guests are visiting your home, your toddler can keep some toys off limits, but the child-guest must have some toys to play with during the visit. Toys that are the least preferred by your toddler are shared with less difficulty. Before the guests arrive, put away toys that may be fought over to avoid or reduce conflict.

Examples of parent statements:

(*Before the guests arrive, to older toddlers with some language ability*)

- "You pick the toys now that you will let Betty play with."
- "You don't have to let Mark play with your big truck, but you have to let him play with some of your toys. Which ones can he play with?"
- "When Maria is here, you need to let her play with your toys and then when you go to visit her at her house, you will get to play with her toys."

(*During a visit when a fight starts*)

- (*To other child*) "I'm sorry, but Tina doesn't feel like sharing this doll today. You may play with this one."
- (*To your own child*) "You need to give Mike a toy for him to play with. It's very important to share some of your toys with guests."

Toddlers are more easily redirected and interested in other toys or activities than older children. If a fight over a toy occurs, try to interest the children in other toys or activities or have the children practice taking turns with direct adult supervision.

Examples of parent statements:

- "You know, it's not much fun to waste play time fighting over toys. Let's go do something else . . . How about. . . ."

- "Okay, we're going to take turns. Anita will go first. (*Time for turn is completed*) "All right, now it's Jesse's turn."

Physically direct or move the children. For example, if the problem is fighting over a turn on a bike, establish who will go first. Remove the first child riding the bike from the bike and place the other child on the bike. Keep the turns very short so waiting for the next turn is less difficult.

Parents should help children learn to share.

CHAPTER 8

Preschool Age

(approximately two-and-one-half to six years of age)

Key Ideas

- Preschool-age children are primarily concerned with developing competence and mastery over daily living skills.

- Peer relationships and social skills become increasingly important, but the main focus is still on the family, especially parents.

- Children's knowledge and understanding of rules and expectations increase faster than their emotional control over their natural impulses and actions.

- Preschoolers do not reliably know the difference between what is real and what is fantasy or pretend.

- Parenting techniques that help children learn from mistakes rather than be afraid of mistakes help children develop responsible behavior.

Important Definitions

1. **Competency:** Competency means being able to do something well. Children naturally want to develop competency. They want to be able to master age-appropriate tasks such as tying their shoes, learning to read, making and keeping friends.

2. **Concrete thinking:** Young children take words literally and can't think in abstract terms or symbols. They are tied to the real, physical world and literal meanings. This very literal thinking is called concrete thinking. An older elementary-age child will understand that "don't cry over spilled milk" is an abstract saying not to be taken literally; a preschooler, however, will think literally that no one

Children naturally want to develop competence.

should cry when milk spills. Preschool-age children need to count out numbers on their fingers because they cannot yet mentally represent numbers with abstract symbols (ten units is represented by the symbol, "10").

3. **Egocentric:** Preschoolers are egocentric in that they cannot look at a situation from another's point of view. This does not mean they cannot express sympathy or compassion.

Young children can be compassionate.

Overview of the Preschool-Age Stage

Preschoolers have learned they are separate people. They focus on developing their self-sufficiency and mastery over daily living skills. Friendships with peers begin to become important. They become increasingly interested in having more say so over decisions affecting them, what happens to them, what they wear, what they do. Thus, most conflicts in this age range are over who will decide what for the child. Preschoolers throw tantrums over what clothes to wear to school and other seemingly trivial situations. They sometimes dig their heels in over a parental directive because to do otherwise would make them feel incompetent.

Young children are growing and changing physically, socially, intellectually, and emotionally at uneven and uncoordinated rates. A child may have mastered many intellectual tasks but may lag behind in emotional self-control. Preschool-age children are frequently frustrated because they understand very well what they cannot yet do on their own or what they cannot have, but are unable to accept disappointment easily. Preschoolers, no matter how smart or how mature for their age,

Expect intense emotions from preschoolers.

are still very young children. Expect them to act with low impulse control, unpredictability, and intense emotionality.

Preschool-age children are egocentric. They cannot understand another person's point of view or perspective. At times they can be very generous, but often preschool-age children are self-centered and concerned only about their own needs. Self-centeredness in this age group is normal and developmentally necessary in order for the child to move from total dependence to independence. You can help your child learn how to balance his or her needs with the needs of others by concentrating on encouraging appropriate behavior rather than on making your child fully understand why certain behaviors are appropriate and others are not.

Even though children in this age group are egocentric, they can be sympathetic and compassionate to others. They can understand that another person is distressed and may try to comfort that individual. However, they still view all situations from their own perspective. If a child sees an adult cry, the child may respond by giving the adult a stuffed animal in an attempt to offer comfort.

Even though egocentric, preschool-age children can be sympathetic.

Preschoolers are egocentric in how they judge what is wrong and how bad the wrongdoing is. They tend to judge how bad something is by how bad the outcome is rather than on the intention behind the behavior. For example, a shelf of toys knocked over accidentally is seen as worse than one toy being knocked off a shelf intentionally. This tendency to judge on the basis of outcome (how much damage) rather than intention (damage caused either on purpose or by accident) is common even up to six or seven years of age.

Preschoolers' egocentrism is also reflected in how they judge their own accountability for a wrongdoing. If a child is hit accidentally by another child, that offense is seen as being as bad as if the child is hit intentionally. However, if the same child accidentally hits another child, he or she will often insist that an apology is not required because the hitting was accidental. You will be more effective when you concentrate on helping your child give the proper responses, whether or not he or she fully comprehends the ethics of the situation. You should state your view of the proper attitude and behavior, but not expect your child to understand fully at this age. You might say, "I know it was just an accident that you ran into Sam with your truck. You still need to say you're sorry even though it was an accident," or "It was just an accident that you bumped into the shelf. I'm glad you didn't get hurt. This is why it's important that we are careful about how fast we move in this room. Now, let's put the toys back on the shelves."

Even though young children are continually learning about consequences (cause and effect), they have not yet mastered logical thinking. This limits their ability to generalize their learning from specific incidents to new situations that may have similar characteristics. They may know not to run off in the grocery store parking lot, but they may not be able to generalize this principle to all parking lots. They cannot consider two concepts at the same time. For example, preschool-age children can sort items by color but they cannot sort items by shape *and* color. They could not put only the square and blue items in a bowl and leave out all items which are not both square and blue. Children begin showing this ability about the age of seven years.

Key Developmental Themes: Developing Initiative and Competency

Having learned they are separate, distinct individuals, preschool-age children can begin working on self-sufficiency. They begin concentrating on developing mastery over the environment, which involves developing competency in daily living, peer friendships, and social skills. A primary intellectual task for this age group is learning about the qualities and properties of things (colors, shapes, textures) and learning about same and different. They are expanding their language skills, imaginative thinking, and pretend play. With a child's increasing self-sufficiency comes increasing demands for control and autonomy over his or her life.

Because being competent is so important, preschoolers need many opportunities to show success. Acknowledgment from adults for their accomplishments, however small, is important for them because it helps them develop initiative and persistence even in the face of frustration. Children will develop initiative and persistence when their efforts and attempts at self-sufficiency and self-expression are respected and praised. Being able to get along well with peers also fosters their sense of competency and sets the stage for having positive relationships with people outside the family.

Peer friendships become more important to preschool-age children.

Implications for Discipline

At this age, children have not only acquired a basic ability to re-member consequences of actions and an increasing desire to do for themselves (autonomy) but they also have low impulse control and an egocentric view of the world. Because preschool-age children are ego-centric, understanding the preschooler's view of a situation is very im-portant when making parenting decisions. Understanding your child's view will help you determine if the misbehavior is a bid for control, a misunderstanding, or a reaction to a perceived disappointment. Know-ing the motivation behind a misbehavior will help you select effective consequences and decide how to approach teaching proper behavior.

Preschoolers respond well to empathy and remember consequences well enough to increasingly restrain themselves from acting on their impulses. They are now more likely to obey a parental request or direc-tive or volunteer to share than when they were toddlers. Their language skills have expanded, allowing them to think beyond their immediate needs. They can recall more easily the benefits of waiting for their im-pulses to be satisfied. Their language skills, however, can be deceiving and can lead a parent to overestimate how much a child truly under-stands. Therefore, try to consider carefully whether or not a misbehavior is the result of the child's youthful misunderstanding of the situation or plain old uncooperativeness.

Unlike toddlers, preschool-age children have the ability to remem-ber the consequences of their actions. However, because of their low impulse control and egocentric thinking, expecting children to stop their impulses just for someone else's benefit is unreasonable. They can ac-cept the rationales for why standards of conduct and rules are in place, but have a very limited understanding of why these rationales have become the agreed upon guidelines for standards of conduct in society. Children will learn to stop their impulses through experiencing conse-quences and seeing their parents model self-control. Consequences that are instructive in nature are very effective in this age group because most misbehavior is out of desire for self-sufficiency or low impulse control.

Preschool-age children are easily distracted and cannot take in long and complicated verbal explanations. Try to be at eye level with your child. Have your child make eye contact with you and give one instruc-tion at a time. Having your child repeat the important point you are making or repeat the directive will help him or her pay attention and will let you know what your child has understood.

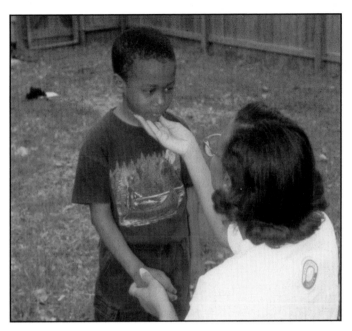

Be at eye level, make eye contact, and give one instruction at a time.

Because preschool-age children can remember consequences consistently but have low impulse control, consequences and behavior change programs can be used to manage misbehavior. General strategies for common misbehaviors are described below. As a demonstration of how to set up a program with preschool-age children, one sample of a detailed behavior-change program for interrupting is at the end of this section. The basic features can be used with other misbehaviors as well.

Common Misbehaviors

- Temper tantrums
- Whining
- Difficulty sharing possessions
- Untruthfulness
- Not asking for permission
- Taking others' possessions
- Bad language
- Interrupting

Temper Tantrums

Preschoolers throw tantrums because they know and remember what they want and still take disappointment hard. As a result, their tantrums are usually more intense and last longer than toddler tantrums. Preschool-age children frequently throw tantrums because they may misunderstand the meaning of words or situations that adults take for granted. A preschool-age child, for example, may not understand that "a pair" means two shoes of the same size for each foot and may throw a tantrum because she or he thinks when a parent says, "You can only have one pair of shoes" that the parent means "You can only have one shoe."

In addition to the strategies used with toddlers, such as empathic statements, or removing yourself from the area, parents can use negative consequences in response to tantrums. Preschoolers have enough memory and knowledge of what consequences will follow which misbehavior (cause-effect relationships) that they can be taught self-control by the enforcement of negative consequences for tantrums and a discussion

Staying calm during a temper tantrum can be very hard.

about why tantrums are unacceptable. This discussion should be held after everyone has calmed down.

Temper tantrums often seem to happen when the parent is pressured, hurried, or in public places. These situations make a child's compliance all the more necessary. When your child is this upset, you may find that staying calm is very hard, especially when your own frustration tolerance is strained.

Temper tantrums in public places are usually the child's bids for the parent to get something like sweets or toys. As with toddlers, parents can simply leave the situation. But leaving a grocery store or cutting short other essential household business errands may be very inconvenient. However, leaving becomes a negative consequence for the child, because leaving eliminates the rewards for the tantrum. Leaving is not a defeat for the parent but shows the parent's refusal to be intimidated by an intense emotional outburst. Leaving without getting anything, especially if proper behavior would have resulted in a treat, teaches children that tantrums are ineffective ways of getting what they want.

When leaving is not an option, taking your child to a private location can help him or her calm down. You can discuss the problem behavior and repeat the predetermined rules or expectations. Preschoolers, like toddlers, may respond to either redirecting or the chance to earn something they want later in exchange for calm behavior in the present.

In some cases, the child has been instructed ahead of time about what behavior is expected and a treat has been offered as a reward for appropriate behavior, but the child throws a tantrum anyway. Parents need to inform the child that the reward has been lost and stick by this decision. If children ultimately earn rewards despite having a temper tantrum, they will learn that there is no real consequence for having a temper tantrum. Tantrums will not only persist, they will intensify. Children will learn to disregard warnings about consequences for their behavior because they know they can always earn back the reward despite throwing a temper tantrum.

Examples of parent statements:

- "I know you want that candy, but we are not getting any sweets today. Please don't ask me again. If you do, you won't get to come with me to the store the next time I go."

- "Before we came, you agreed to follow the rules. We agreed that if you followed the rules, you would get an extra bedtime story tonight. You have lost being able to have an extra story." (*Expect an intense, outraged response, but stick to your decision and make empathic comments*) "... I know you're mad. I'm not changing my mind. It's hard to lose something you want."

Thinking about some possible causes of the tantrum may help you find that the motivation behind the tantrum is due to a misunderstanding. Understanding the motivation will help you think of how to manage the situation in a way that safeguards your child's self-esteem without allowing misbehavior to be rewarded. Sometimes the tantrum is based on a misunderstanding and the child would have good reason to be upset if her or his view of the situation had been accurate. A consequence for this tantrum would likely be counterproductive. You would be more effective by focusing on helping your child have a better understanding for future reference. In the misunderstanding given above about what "pair" meant, the parent could make sure the child understands fully that "pair" means two of something. Over time, children will be able to learn the importance of checking out their understanding of a situation before they jump to a wrong conclusion.

Example of parent statement:

- "I didn't know you thought pair meant just one shoe. A pair always means two of something. See, we were both thinking the same thing: that you needed a shoe for each foot. But, you were upset because you thought I was going to get just one shoe for you and I was upset because I couldn't understand why you were so upset. You can see how important it is to make sure we understand each other. We certainly don't need to fight about something we agree on!"

Ignoring a temper tantrum and letting it run its course is an effective strategy because the child does not receive any reinforcement for the tantrum. You can ignore tantrums in situations where the child will be safe through the duration of the tantrum such as when you are at home. You may want to occasionally make empathic statements so that your child does not feel so ignored that she or he escalates the tantrum in order to get your attention. You need to judge whether or not the empathic statements are helping your child calm down or are reinforcing the tantrum. If you feel strongly that ignoring the temper tantrum is not helpful, you can give preschoolers the option of calming down or going to time-out (to calm down).

Examples of parent statements:

- "I know you're upset about not getting to go to the store with Daddy, but you need to calm yourself down.
- "I know you're upset. You have a choice of calming down in time-out or staying where you are. I'm going to set the timer to help you keep track of the time. You need to be calm by the time the timer goes off."

Hint: Set the timer for a little more time than you think your child needs so he or she can feel successful about "beating the clock."

Whining

Whining, an especially irritating behavior from children, begins as a natural expression of the emotions caused by frustration and anger. If children get what they want when they whine, they learn they can force a parent to do things by showing anger in this way. Parents can train children not to whine by refusing outright to give them what they want until they ask in a normal voice or by refusing to give them what they want when they whine. Parents need to be consistent in their refusal to cave in to a child's demands when the child whines. If whining works every now and then, it becomes an even stronger habit. Parents should not respond with an irritated tone because that sounds the same as whining to children.

Tell the child to use a regular voice. Say what words should be said and model the proper tone of voice for making a request. After hearing this several times, children usually only need the cue, "Please use a regular voice," to remember how to ask appropriately. When children use a regular tone of voice, they should be complimented on their grown-up way of asking.

Examples of parent statements:

- "I want you to ask in this tone of voice. Say it like this . . ." (*Parent says what the child should say, modeling the proper tone of voice, volume, and manners required to meet the definition of "regular voice"*).
- "You need to ask in a regular voice and say, 'Please.'"
- "Please, use a regular voice."
- "I'm so glad you used a regular voice. It's so much nicer to hear, and I feel so much more like getting you what you've asked for."

Whining is caused by frustration, fatigue, or anger.

Difficulty Sharing Possessions

Preschool-age children can share even when sharing is forced on them. Children this age want to play with other children, which often means sharing. Problems for this age group with sharing typically have different causes than for toddlers. Problems happen more often when only one especially desirable toy is available or when a child feels that his or her territory is being invaded. Sometimes children will fight over toys because they feel competitive.

When sharing is a problem for preschoolers, use the same basic approach as with toddlers (see chapter 7). One added feature is that preschoolers can often respond to basic reason and parental rules about sharing. Parents can explain in simple terms why sharing is important without trying to make the child feel guilty for his or her feelings. Although preschoolers are egocentric, they can be led to understand how they would feel if another child refused to share with them. Unfortunately, understanding how they would feel if the tables were turned does not always lead to gracious sharing. Being made to share, however, and being given an explanation of the value and benefits of sharing does

Preschoolers can understand the benefits of sharing.

help them learn how to share more willingly. If for no other reason, they share because they want their parents' approval.

Examples of parent statements:

- "You need to let Tom play with some of your toys. I know you want Tom to come and play with you. If you don't share your toys with him, he won't feel like coming over anymore and then you would be sad because you wouldn't have him to play with."
- "Think about how you would feel if you were at Mary's house and she wouldn't let you play with any of her toys. You would feel sad. If you don't share, Mary will feel sad. You like to play with Mary, but she won't want to play with you if you don't share."

Untruthfulness

Untruths in preschoolers are not conscious, malicious attempts at deception. Preschool-age children cannot reliably tell the difference between reality and fantasy. At this age, children still have very short memories and some of their denial of truth is due to genuine forgetfulness. Their untruthful statements are usually wishes being confused with reality or naive attempts to avoid an unpleasant chore or punishment. Even so, preschoolers still need to be corrected in these situations. Corrections teach them how to be responsible and how to admit mistakes.

If children persist in claiming their version is accurate, parents can calmly tell children what the parent's view of the situation is but not argue with them about it. Focus on reexplaining the rule and why the rule exists. Tell the child to follow through on the directive regardless of what the child thinks the real truth is.

Examples of parent statements:

- "You are holding the crayons in your hands. I know you drew on the wall. Don't tell me that you did not do something when you did it. It is very important to tell the truth when we make mistakes and take responsibility for what we do. Now you need to scrub that off. I'll go get the soap and water."

- "I know you'd like to believe that Carlos was the only one playing with your toys, but you were playing with them, too. It's
  time to put the toy away now." (*If child continues to argue*) "You
  know, these toys are yours, and no matter who plays with them,
  you're the one who's responsible for them. If no one else helps
  put them up even if they got them out, it's your job to see that
  they are put up. If any of your friends play with your toys and
  then won't help you pick them up when it's time, then they
  aren't being good friends to you and you shouldn't invite them
  over to play unless they agree to help you pick up."
- "I can tell you got into the cookies. Please don't tell me you
  didn't when you know you did. The rule is that you wait until
  after dinner to eat cookies. I also don't want you climbing up on
  the counter. You might fall and get hurt. Because you got into
  the cookies without permission, you will not get any dessert
  tonight or tomorrow either. Next time you tell me you didn't do
  something when you did, you will have even more privileges
  taken away—some for what you did wrong and some more for
  not telling me the truth about it."

Not Asking for Permission

Parents encourage their children to do things for themselves. Although children's ability to be self-sufficient grows rapidly, it is still
limited. Their desire for independence is strong, but their physical abilities and judgment are not well developed. Few preschool-age children
willfully disregard rules simply out of disrespect to their parents. The
main reasons why preschoolers do not ask for permission first include
low impulse control, a desire for competency, and true confusion about
what activities require parental permission.

Consequences that are instructional in nature are very effective for
these situations. For example, the child wants to pour his own glass of
milk. The child does not ask permission first because he wants to "do it
himself." He spills the milk. Making the child clean up the spill as a
consequence instead of scolding him helps the child understand better
why his parents want him to be willing to accept their help. Cleaning up
is not fun and the child learns that asking and getting help is better than
spending time cleaning up a mess.

Preschoolers are able to understand simple explanations and consider the importance of rules before acting. Although not as strong a motivator as a consequence, giving your child the rationale behind why permission is needed in each particular situation will also help him or her learn when to ask for permission or for help. When children believe they can get hurt, they can recall this possibility and stop their impulses. If they realize that rules are helpful to them, they can recall this positive experience to help them follow a rule.

Examples of parent statements:

- "I know you want to do things for yourself. I'm glad you want to do things for yourself. Sometimes you are still going to need

Preschoolers learn more when consequences also teach appropriate behavior.

to ask me for help. Like now. The milk container was too heavy for you because it was full. Here's a sponge to clean up the spill. Next time, check with me first, please."

- "Climbing on this shelf is very dangerous. It's not safe. The shelf may tip over and fall on top of you. Come get me when you want something on the top shelf."
- "I put that clay on the top shelf because you still need my help when you play with it. Now you need to put this all away. Because you didn't ask first, you can't play with the clay for three days."
- "It's not okay for you to get into my makeup. It belongs to me. You'll ruin it if you play with it. You need to ask me permission before you get into any of my things. You wouldn't like it if someone played with your toys without you saying it was okay, especially if that someone broke your toys. If this happens again or you get into something else of mine without permission, I'm going to put up all your dolls for three days. You need to learn to respect other people's property. Ask first."

Taking Others' Possessions

Preschool-age children have a very basic understanding of ownership. They understand that some things are theirs and some things belong to other people. However, they are still driven by their immediate impulses. Very young preschoolers may take something that is not theirs because they still do not know or remember at the time that they need to ask the owner for permission and because they also have low impulse control. Older preschoolers, about five years and older, are aware when they are taking something that does not belong to them. They may even feel guilty but are so driven by their impulses they cannot stop themselves.

Children respond well to a simple statement of the rule and a brief explanation. Asking them or reminding them of how they would feel if someone took their things also helps them understand why the rule is important and how the rule benefits them as well.

Examples of parent statements:

- "These toys belong to Tamara. The toys need to stay here. You can play with them again the next time you come."
- "We don't take things that don't belong to us. You wouldn't want anyone to take your toys. If one of your friends took your toys you would feel angry and sad. You wouldn't trust that friend anymore. You might not even want that friend to come over to play because you couldn't trust that your toys would stay at home."

Bad Language

Children are exposed to socially inappropriate and sometimes vulgar language at very young ages. Children may learn and use words that are unacceptable in their family. They may also use words that are not vulgar themselves but are rude in their intended meaning such as "doo-doo head." Often children do not know what these words mean and are simply imitating what they have heard.

Parents need to decide what words are acceptable within their family and then teach their children the acceptable words and contexts for them. A child may tell his parents he needs to go "doo-doo" because the word describes an important bodily function. However, he is not allowed to call his sister a "doo-doo head" because in this context the word is vulgar. Give children acceptable substitute words or phrases.

Parents also need to make sure their own language models the word choices they want their children to use. If a child overhears a parent use a swear word, the parent can apologize to the child, acknowledge the mistake, and restate that the word is not an acceptable word.

Examples of parent statements:

- "I know that in Mara's family, her parents do not mind that word. Different families have different ideas about what words are okay to say. In our family, we don't think that is a nice word and I don't want you to say it. You can say . . . (*offer a substitute*) instead."
- "I'm sorry I lost my temper and said a bad word. It's not a nice word, and I should not have said it. I will try very hard not to

use it again. I hope you won't use it either. It would have been better if . . .

    a. I would have said (*substitute*) instead."

    b. I had not said anything at all."

- (*To a guest child*): "In our family we don't use that word . . .

    a. We say (*substitute word*) instead."

    b. When you're with us, it's not okay to use that word. If you're angry, you need to (*offer the alternative*) . . .

        - Let me know what you're upset about."
        - Come get me; I'll help you both work it out."

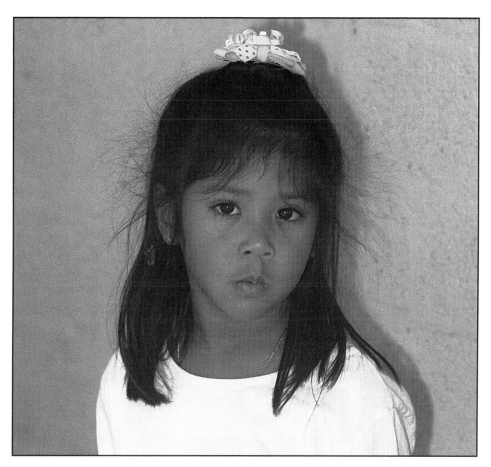

Children often imitate what they have heard.

Interrupting

Preschool-age children are quite fluent in their language skills. They can talk at length about many ideas and ask many, many questions. Their low impulse control and egocentricism make waiting for their turn to talk very difficult.

First, teach your child a nonverbal signal such as a gentle two-finger tap on your arm to use when he or she wants to say something. If a signal is used at your child's school, use the same signal at home. When your child uses the signal properly, let him or her know the signal was received either by verbally acknowledging the signal or with a nonverbal hug or similar gesture. Compliment your child for being polite and patient. When your child forgets to use the signal, remind him or her to use the signal and wait his or her turn. Let your child talk very soon after the signal, even if only for a brief time.

Compliment your child for being polite and patient.

Examples of parent statements:

- "Thank you for letting me know you want to say something."
- "Thank you for letting me know you want to say something. It will be your turn to talk in a few minutes."
- "You are being so patient and polite. Let me finish this story and then you can ask me your question."

With siblings or groups of children, having a tangible object like a ball, artificial flower, or a wooden spoon to hold during their turn to speak can help them take turns. Whoever is holding the object is allowed to speak. The object is handed over to the next speaker when it's his or her turn. Because children are very concrete, seeing the object helps them remember the rule about one person speaking at a time. Also, the object is proof of whose turn it is if a dispute arises. The amount of time for talking should be equitably divided between children.

Application of a Behavior Change Program

When a misbehavior is at such a high level that children need more direct teaching, parents can use a behavior change program. Review the general description of behavior change programs described in chapter 4. You can set up a program several ways to help children learn new behaviors. One way involves earning tokens for behaving properly; another involves losing tokens for misbehaving.

Sample Program to Reduce Interrupting

Before starting, the program should be completely discussed with and agreed to by the child. Start off with just one situation where the child interrupts. For example, the program will only be in effect when parents are talking with each other or the program will only be in effect when a parent is talking to friends or to teachers. To prevent the child from secretly adding tokens, tokens should not be too similar to items easily available to the child. Toy or real poker chips work well.

Example of parent statement:

- "You know how it's hard for you to wait for your turn to talk so you end up interrupting us a lot? We want to help you learn how to wait your turn. It's important for everyone to have some time to talk without being interrupted. We've come up with a way for you to practice waiting for your turn to talk. Every time Dad and I are talking and you want to say something, use the signal. If you can wait for thirty seconds without interrupting, you will get one of these tokens. When you earn enough tokens, you will be able to trade them in for something you want."

Earning Tokens

Although earning tokens for waiting patiently is a positive approach, it won't work with every child. Children who are basically eager to please seem to respond well to an earning type of structure.

In this structure, parents keep a number of tokens within immediate reach. In the beginning, the child is first told how long she or he must wait without interrupting in order to earn a token. The child then earns the token after having waited for that length of time. For example, if the child can earn one token for thirty seconds of waiting while parents are talking with each other, the parents would give the child a token after every thirty-second time period in which the child has not interrupted them. As the child's self-control improves, the length of time is increased. Always compliment the child for waiting when handing the child the token. Praise is a very powerful reinforcer.

Taking Away Tokens

This structure follows the basic principles of response cost outlined in chapter 6. Parents start the day by giving the child a full set of tokens. Each time the child interrupts, a token is taken away. The exact amount of tokens needed to make up a full set depends on how often a child interrupts and how long during that day the child will be in situations where interrupting is a problem.

Before starting the program, parents should estimate how many tokens their child will lose due to interrupting. The best way to estimate the number of tokens is to tally the number of interruptions for one week keeping track of whether or not the number changes depending on the day of the week or the situation.

To maximize success and motivation, parents should give their children enough tokens initially so that children should have several left at the end of the day. Otherwise children may become too discouraged and stop trying. As children improve, parents should reduce the number of tokens they hand out at the beginning of the day.

You and your child should decide together what kind of rewards or privileges can be earned and how many tokens will be needed to exchange for these rewards. For example, ten tokens can be exchanged for one choice of a home video rental. Set the number of tokens needed for exchanges low in the beginning and then raise the exchange rate as the number of tokens a child keeps increases. Through trial and error, find a

Remember to combine praise with tokens.

balance between work and incentive, that is, a fair balance between making your child wait patiently long enough, and often enough, and giving your child incentive enough for working on patience.

Other Factors

When planning a behavior reinforcement program it is always wise for parents to ask themselves why the misbehavior may be emerging at this time and how it fits with the developmental themes of the child's age. For the preschool-age child, other factors that may contribute to interrupting are modeling by other family members (the child sees other family members frequently interrupt each other) or lack of opportunities for individual attention.

CHAPTER 9

Elementary Age

(six to twelve years of age)

Key Ideas

- Elementary-age children continue to develop their competency and autonomy.

- Elementary-age children are beginning to think more abstractly but are still tied to the real, physical world.

- Peers become very important, especially same gender friendships.

- By age eight, most children are able to distinguish reality from fantasy and fiction.

Important Definitions

1. **Abstract thinking:** Abstract thinking means being able to think in general principles beyond or apart from a specific example. A proverb is an example of abstract thinking because the proverb refers to a general principle, not to the literal meaning of the words. The symbols for numbers are also examples of abstract thinking. The symbol "10" represents a quantity of ten units. Words are another form of abstract thinking because words represent real objects but are not the objects themselves.

2. **Relativism:** Relativism means that more than one explanation or perspective exists depending on circumstances or a person's viewpoint. Elementary-age children understand that several possible reasons or explanations can be behind one specific behavior. They begin to move from thinking their perspective is the only possible perspective, to understanding that people can have different perceptions, different emotional reactions, and different motivations.

Elementary-age children develop more specific ideas about who they are.

3. **Self-concept and self-esteem:** Self-concept is our idea of who and what we are, our identity. Self-esteem is the personal judgment people make about their value as individuals and is based, in part, on the individual's self-concept. Theoretically, two people could have very similar self-concepts but one person could have a high self-esteem and the other a low self-esteem.

4. **Gender identity:** Children learn at an early age which gender they are. Children then develop more specific ideas about what characteristics define either masculinity or femininity within their culture. These ideas are based in children's genetic makeup and in their experience of how men and women behave.

Self-concept is our idea of who and what we are.

Overview of the Elementary-Age Stage

From about age six to twelve, children become increasingly responsive to reason and better able to delay their immediate impulses. Unlike preschoolers, elementary-age children are beginning to understand more abstract concepts such as math symbols, abstract sayings, general principles, and basic logic. They can better understand abstract concepts like trust, responsibility, and courtesy, although true abstract thinking does not come about until adolescence and adulthood. They not only understand rules better, but also want to know why a rule is important instead of just following the rule because they have been told to do so. They begin to understand that sayings such as, "There's no use crying over spilled milk," are not to be taken literally, but refer to a general way of thinking about events. Elementary-age children can now begin to make generalizations from a specific learning situation to new situations. For example, they can conclude on their own that if ice melts, then all frozen foods will change as they thaw. They can reason that if they get hurt from jumping without thinking first about safety, then thinking before acting as a general principle is a good idea.

Being able to think abstractly is a critical development for children. Abstract thought allows them to understand their world in more complex ways. Their logical reasoning and capacity for concentration, attention, and memory increases substantially. Children at this age begin to form ideas about cause-and-effect relationships and abstract general principles based on their specific experiences. Abstract thought helps children consider the predictable and possible consequences of their actions before acting. Abstract reasoning is a building block in the development of imagination, creativity, and problem-solving.

The capacity for relativism combined with abstract reasoning increases the child's ability to learn through observing the experience of another. Children no longer rely on direct personal experience alone for learning. They can see what consequences happen to another child for a behavior and understand that those consequences could also apply to them if they choose to behave similarly. They can think, "Jesse jumped off the picnic table without looking and cut his forehead. That could happen to me if I jump off the picnic table without looking. I should look before I leap."

Children in this age range are discovering who they are and establishing their unique, personal identity. A child's self-concept is not necessarily an accurate inventory or appraisal of their characteristics, abilities, and circumstances. Self-concept is their unique, personal assessment of these characteristics that may be accurate but is more likely to be an over- or underestimation. Children build up their self-concept and self-esteem through interactions with significant others and the physical environment.

For elementary-age children where developing a sense of competence is of prime importance, accurate self-concept and good self-esteem are built through accurate feedback and opportunities to demonstrate mastery and achieve success. Mastery and success do not come without effort. The process of achieving mastery and success involves trying,

Elementary-age children use more observation and reason and depend less on direct experience to make decisions.

failing, regrouping, and trying again. This is the route to competence and a durable self-esteem.

Self-concept is also subject to change as different experiences are acquired. For example, a child's abilities and physical characteristics change with maturity and his or her self-concept is modified accordingly. A child's self-concept is also influenced by changes in the environment and changes in the people in his or her life. For instance, with a change in schools, a child may discover he or she is no longer the best soccer player on the team. Or, previously unrecognized talent, like artistic skill, may blossom under a supportive teacher. Even though much of an elementary-age child's self-concept depends on feedback from peer relationships, positive relationships with adults both inside and outside of the family remain crucial to the child's healthy self-esteem.

Becoming aware of the unique combination of features that make up a personality involves identifying preferences as well as strengths and limitations. Having a variety of experiences helps children explore preferences and test their talents and limitations. This process of discovery naturally involves learning by trial and error, which can be both frustrating and embarrassing for them. When children change their mind often, about likes and dislikes, they are showing signs of exploration and learning, not immaturity.

During this stage, peer friendships become extremely important. Children want to fit in and belong to a supportive group of same-age companions. Fitting in with a peer group and having good social skills becomes critical to a child's positive self-concept and self-esteem. Trying to fit in while simultaneously trying to demonstrate and receive recognition for competence can cause children in this age group to become quite competitive.

Competitiveness is a natural and valuable motivation, but needs to be tempered with a reasonable acceptance of other children's successes and talents. When faced with competition, some children will withdraw from interaction as a way of reducing the risk of criticism or rejection. Overly competitive behavior and overly shy behavior are both attempts to preserve self-esteem in a naturally competitive social environment and both lead to negative outcomes for children. The sometimes harsh feedback from peers about either of these styles can help children learn what is acceptable to their contemporaries and what is not. Excessive or continuous criticism or rejection by peers, however, can be damaging.

Peer acceptance and same gender relationships grow in importance.

Elementary-age children's ability to develop friendships is supported by both their abstract reasoning ability and their move from egocentric thinking to relativism, which allows them to understand other people's points of view. The children can begin to consider how people could interpret an event (taking a playmate's toy without permission) in a way that leads them to an angry response (yelling and striking out), which in turn leads to negative consequences (hurt feelings, a fight, punishment). This ability to see things from another person's view allows them to adjust their behavior based on their understanding of another person's attitudes, feelings, and motivations. These cognitive developments increase the child's capacity for empathy and social judgment, which are the foundations of social skill and effective personal relationships.

During the elementary-age period, children also form their ideas about their own gender identity. Children are mostly interested in friendships with playmates of the same gender and this preference helps them develop their concepts of masculinity and femininity. While gender identity is influenced by the cultural context of the child, it is more specifically shaped by the primary role models encountered in daily life: mother, father, siblings, teachers, coaches. These key people provide models for common interests and preferences that may distinguish masculine from feminine. They also model core attitudes, values, and ethics that can become associated with each gender. A child of a compassionate father can believe that a compassionate male is masculine; a child of an assertive mother can believe that an assertive female is feminine.

Key Developmental Themes: Refining Competency and Strengthening Autonomy

As with preschool-age children, elementary-age children are also very concerned about being competent and recognized as such by their families and peers. Most of the time, the desire to be competent and be recognized as competent motivates children to follow rules and cooperate with adult expectations. Elementary-age children still need a great deal of praise and acknowledgment of their efforts and accomplishments because they face increasingly difficult academic tasks and social situations. When effort is praised, children learn to persist longer and have more realistic expectations of what they need to do to be competent and successful.

Implications for Discipline

Elementary-age children are beginning to think abstractly and learn through reasoning, logic, and observation of others. However, trial and error and direct experience with consequences continue to be their main methods of learning. Thus, a child's desire to be competent and be recognized as such can lead to misbehavior such as noncompliance and argumentativeness. Challenging rules and parental authority and experiencing the consequences of failing to exercise good judgment are very important ways children test their competence. Unlike preschoolers, your elementary-age child may press for a more complete, logical explanation of a decision you've made. This can be both frustrating and time consuming. When possible, try to *briefly* spell out the logic of your decisions and enforce compliance even if your child continues to disagree after the explanation. Giving a single, clear explanation shows the child that parental decisions are based on reasonable and consistent principles rather than on a whim.

Praise helps children persist at difficult tasks.

Often, children will not fully understand why a parental request, rule, or a point of view is valid unless they attempt to negotiate to have their way. As children become more able to use abstract reasoning and relativistic thinking, their verbal challenges to parental authority become more sophisticated, persistent, and forceful. They learn that combining reason with strong emotional expression can be effective in getting what they want. This can wear parents down.

Children can also understand and use sarcasm. Words, gestures, and tone of voice can now be used by them in an aggressive way to assert control or get even. For elementary-age children, learning to negotiate with others is crucial. However, they often negotiate by arguing, talking back, and using sarcasm. Being able to control one's life is a natural and good urge. However, children need to learn how to negotiate in a positive way to show they can exercise reasonable judgment and to earn their parents' trust in making more of their own decisions.

Elementary-age children's ability to learn through abstract thinking and reasoning can be used and supported when they are corrected for misbehavior. While setting limits, give your child specific reasons why the behavior is unacceptable and ask him or her to consider how the behavior has affected others. Shame and humiliation from disrespectful scolding by adults can damage a child's self-esteem as well as the parent-child relationship. Being humiliated by another person, especially a loved one, only breeds resentment and does not motivate anyone to change problematic behavior. When children feel disrespected, insulted, or shamed, they stop listening to the main theme about why the behavior should not be repeated. Harsh reprimands also increase a child's desire to conceal mistakes or misdeeds and create some of the same problems as does physical punishment.

Harsh reprimands and shaming teach children to use humiliation and strong, negative emotional displays as a way of intimidating and dominating others. Children's growing cognitive abilities allow them to understand the deeper implications of words that parents use and the implicit messages that are conveyed through the parent's tone of voice and facial gestures. As children's cognitive abilities grow, so does their ability to follow complex examples of communication set by parents. If parents use humiliation to win control then children will use it as well.

Children of this age often do (and rightly so) feel badly when they have caused harm or misbehaved. When children feel badly because they understand how their actions have hurt a good relationship or interfered with being truly competent, then they can be motivated to change for positive reasons and not out of fear of punishment or blind obedience. Strong expressions of negative emotion and sarcasm are naturally provocative for both children and parents, and interactions can quickly escalate into angry exchanges. Parents may find it hard not to respond in kind, but will be more effective when they remain calm and avoid judgmental, derogatory, or sarcastic remarks in discussions about misbehavior.

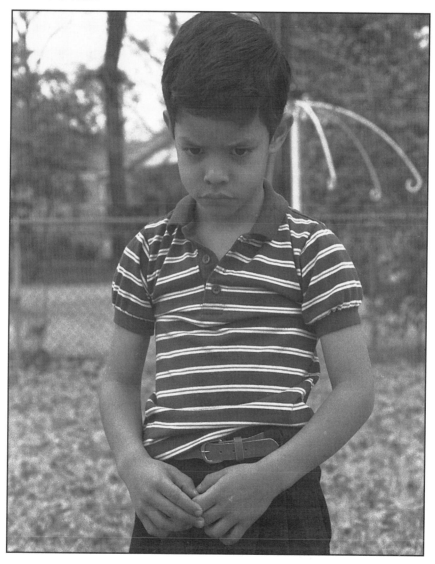

Harsh, disrespectful reprimands can damage
the parent-child relationship.

Common Misbehaviors

- Talking back, sassiness, arguing, sarcasm
- Teasing, making fun of others, bragging
- Stealing
- Bad language
- Untruthfulness

Talking Back, Sassiness, Arguing, Sarcasm

Children's natural drive for autonomy combined with better emotional control, abstract reasoning, and relativistic thinking makes their communication skills increasingly sophisticated. Talking back, sassiness, arguing, and sarcasm are sophisticated but also provocative forms of communication. Many parents find their elementary-age children quite quarrelsome and sassy. Children in this age group argue and talk back in an effort to get their way, in part because they *are* more mature. They have developed better control over their emotions, and what would usually trigger a temper tantrum in a preschooler will now trigger arguing in an elementary-age child. This does not feel like a big improvement to most parents. However, for a child, using words instead of immediately acting on emotions is a big step in the direction of maturity and increasing self-control.

Why do children resort to talking back, sarcasm, and argumentativeness? These behaviors are all forms of verbal aggression; expressions of anger; and attempts to dominate, get even, or avoid being controlled. The main reasons include:

- Being tired, frustrated, or unhappy
- Being intimidated by other children or seeing others use intimidation to gain power
- Having enough abstract thinking skills to know that most rules are based on parental judgment and discretion and are not based on absolute rules like the laws of the physical world
- Having a desire for more autonomy and control but having limited negotiation skills

Sometimes children argue, talk back, or use sarcasm because they are tired, frustrated, or unhappy. At these times, the behavior is more a reflection of a current mood than a basic disrespect of the parent's authority. Children often pick up their styles of arguing or sarcasm from peers without fully realizing how powerfully provocative and offensive their tone and words can be. Argumentativeness or sarcasm is often the first sign that a child is being teased or intimidated in some setting. This possibility should be explored.

Parents are often provoked by a child's sassiness and usually find it difficult to control their own reactions. Parents may be able to shift the interaction from one of conflict to one of problem-solving if they can hold their temper and inquire into their child's mood. For example, if the child is arguing because she or he is in a bad mood from being teased at school, the parent and child will get off track if the parent simply delivers a negative consequence for arguing. If the parent finds out what happened to make the child feel bad, then the parent can discuss the child's experience in a supportive way, make suggestions on better ways to handle being in a bad mood (have the child rehearse talking about the upsetting event for example), and apply consequences if indicated.

Example of parent statement:

- "You are really arguing with me today. You seem upset. Did something happen today to make you feel bad?" (*Child tells parent about having a bad day and they discuss that situation*) "You know, we all get in bad moods from time to time, but it's still important for you to not take it out on others. The next time you have a bad day, let me know right away. It'll be better for all of us if we talk about what's bothering you instead of you giving me a hard time."

Many arguments between parents and children have to do with rules and chores. Elementary-age children have enough abstract thinking ability to know that many rules are based on parental discretion. Children also realize that many rules are relative or dependent upon circumstances. For example, they see different rules in different families. Bedtime can be 8:00 PM or 9:00 PM depending on what different parents decide is right for their own family. Bedtime is not an absolute like the laws of the physical world (such as gravity). Therefore, children see that home rules are potentially changeable. Children argue, in part, because they know that many rules can change if the person enforcing the rules decides to change them.

Examples of parent statements:

- "I'm not going to change my mind. Think about what you're doing and ask yourself if it's going to get you what you want."
- "I know you want more privileges and that you think you can handle more freedom to make your own decisions. Arguing with me about the rules instead of discussing them with me doesn't help me believe that you can handle more freedom."
- "You need to think of a respectful way of telling me you're angry about the rules. I don't insult you when I'm angry with

As abstract reasoning develops, children may become argumentative.

you and I expect you to remember to disagree respectfully, especially with me. If you want more privileges you need to show me you know how to be respectful to me when we disagree."

- "I am getting very tired of how much you argue with me about so many things. All this arguing makes me grouchy."

Parents should look for a pattern in how and when the talking back occurs. Consider why the behavior is emerging at that time. Have your elementary-age child define what talking back or being sassy means to him or her. You should also describe what these behaviors mean to you. Be sure to include a description about the tone of voice, gestures, and word choices. Encourage your child to clarify his or her own view about the reason for talking back or being sassy. Helping your child put views and motivations into words serves several important purposes. First, the child's explanation provides important information about the child's general attitude. Second, the explanation often reveals key factors that bring about the misbehavior. Third, the process of accounting for his or her own behavior helps a child gain insight, understanding, and self-control.

You can then have a detailed conversation with your child about the reasons why talking back or sassiness is not appropriate or useful. Include an explanation of the importance of negotiating respectfully and accepting disappointment without too much complaining. Three main reasons elementary-age children can understand include:

- *Morality:* The golden rule—do unto others as you would have them do unto you.
- *Responsibility:* Parents have legitimate responsibilities that require children to accept their parents' decisions and rules for the good of the whole family.
- *Practicality:* People who know how to respectfully negotiate and know when to cooperate instead of complain get more of what they want. People are more willing to cooperate with them.

Giving your child specific examples of more positive ways to negotiate for what they want is very helpful. For example, take three recent occasions when your child argued or talked back and role-play these situations with the child. Begin by having your child pretend to argue or talk back to you. Then guide him or her through a scenario in which he or she expresses an opinion or request in a positive way.

Examples of parent statements:

- "If you want other people to respect you and your feelings, then even when you're mad, you should let them know that you are respecting their feelings. When you are sarcastic or talk back, you are being disrespectful of them and their feelings."
- "I know you get disappointed when you don't get to do something you want to do. When I say, 'No,' I'm not trying to be mean or frustrate you. I'd like you to remember that I have good reasons why I say 'No.' You may not always understand the reasons and you may not even think they are good reasons, but I'm responsible for you and I have to do what I think is best."
- "Talking back and being sassy to someone just makes that person mad. You end up with less of what you want. It's important for you to learn how to respectfully disagree and how to accept not always getting your way."
- "It's OK for you to ask for things and it's even OK for you to negotiate for things. It's not OK to argue and give me a hard time when I say, 'No.' I want you to learn how to negotiate instead of argue. I want you to learn how to take 'No' for an answer without giving me such a hard time. I want to help you practice how to negotiate instead of argue and learn how to accept disappointment better."

Teasing, Making Fun of Others, Bragging

Elementary-age children are very concerned about being competent and fitting in with peers. Frequently, children in this age range tease, make fun of others, or brag because of concerns they have about their own talents, not because they are mean. A child who may be worried about not being smart may brag or tease another child in an effort to stop feeling so anxious about his or her own intelligence.

This problem can be magnified when children are in groups. Because fitting in with a peer group is very important, anyone who does not appear to fit in causes many children to worry about their own acceptance by peers. Bragging and verbally attacking others, particularly a child who does not fit in, is a way children defend themselves against worries about their own abilities or characteristics. Thinking, even unconsciously, "At least I'm not as bad off as them," soothes some of the worry and protects their own self-esteem. Even though they are psychologically understandable, these behaviors must stop for the child's long-term best interest as well as for the best interest of the child who is the brunt of the teasing. Children who are excessive in bragging and teasing have difficulty forming good friendships and working relationships with others as adults.

Teasing may be a defense against self-doubt.

Parents can help children work on these issues by talking with their child about what they have heard or observed. They can remind their child how other people should be treated and gently inquire if something might be of concern to the child. Parents can also have their children think about how it would make them feel if they were being teased. Parents can also tell their child what this behavior usually says about the person doing it, if they think this may help the child develop more self-control. Parents should avoid guilt-inducing tones or word choices. Use a matter-of-fact, educational manner. If the parent determines that a whole group of children are teasing a child, then more direct action is called for, such as meetings with the school or other parents.

Examples of parent statements:

- "You know, I heard from Leah's dad that you called her a loser last night when your team lost. Can you tell me what you were thinking or feeling when you called her that?" (*Some discussion of the child's mood at the time*) "You are all on the same team and you need to support your teammates. No one is perfect and everyone makes mistakes. You know our family does not approve of name-calling."
- "You know sometimes when you call someone else a loser that means you are really worried that you are a loser yourself."
- "I know you like to get the highest grades possible. I'm proud that you work hard at school. It's good to be proud about yourself, but it's not very thoughtful of other people's feelings when you brag about how good you are at something even if it's true. It's one thing to let people know what you do well, it's another to rub it in their faces. Bragging makes other people feel bad and angry. You're not a better person just because you can do something better than another person. Trying to make yourself feel better by making someone else feel bad about not doing as well as you is wrong. Other kids aren't going to want to be with you if you act like you're better than them."

Stealing

Elementary-age children do know when they are stealing. They are not confused about ownership. Children in this age range may steal for a number of reasons:

- The temptation was too great
- Their parent has refused to purchase the item for them
- They want something they cannot afford
- Peer pressure (for popularity or attention)
- They feel sad and think that having more material things will help
- They are angry about some other issue and stealing is a way of getting back for some perceived unfairness or striking back at authority

Parents are understandably upset when they discover that their child has stolen. Parents often feel humiliated and worried about their child's moral character. Speaking calmly to a child can be very difficult. Parents will help their child more if they refrain from harsh reprimands such as calling their child names, like "thief," or making gross generalizations like, "I can never trust you out of my sight again," or "You're going to end up in jail for the rest of your life."

Parents need to understand the motivation behind the theft. They need to spend time understanding their child's feelings and perspective and then address the root problem. Once parents have a good idea of the motivation, they can begin helping the child find socially appropriate ways of handling these feelings. Stealing will stop if the root causes are addressed, if the child experiences negative consequences, and if the child realizes how stealing actually harms both parties.

Examples of parent statements:

- "Julie, I was wondering what you were thinking about when you took that lipstick from the store."
- "I'm having a hard time understanding how come you took that watch. Will you tell me how come you took it?"
- "I know you don't want to talk about this. I know you're embarrassed and upset. You even look angry. But I am curious how come you took that toy soldier."

Typically, children experience a substantial amount of shame when their theft is discovered, when they are forced to admit it publicly, or when they have to make restitution. Parents do not need to add more shame. If children find the shame too painful, they may not be able to learn from the experience. They may pretend not to be bothered or be unable to even think about the reasons why they stole and how to change their behavior.

Few children steal more than a couple of times. If stealing becomes frequent, professional consultation is recommended. Stealing can become a difficult habit to break with severe consequences beyond the

Children usually feel ashamed when they are caught stealing.

control of the family. Professional consultation may help uncover the underlying reasons behind stealing and help children learn positive ways to satisfy more of their needs.

Giving the child a serious but educational consequence will reinforce the value of honesty. Regardless of the reasons for stealing, children need to be held accountable for their actions. If your child has shoplifted, he or she should be made to go back to the store to return the stolen item, offer payment or compensation, and apologize to the manager for the theft. When children steal from family, friends, schools, or churches, they should also apologize and return or offer compensation for stolen items. Consequences for stealing should outweigh the potential payoff for stealing. Children may need additional consequences to the ones mentioned above. For example, children can be required to do "community service" for the injured party or asked to write a report on the importance of trust and honesty.

Examples of parent statements:

- "It's not OK to take things that aren't yours. You wouldn't like it if someone stole your toys or clothes. If you steal things, people won't trust you. They won't want to be with you. It's not fair to other people if you take something that belongs to them. They have either worked hard to earn it or it was a gift to them from someone else. You need to go back to the store and apologize to the manager. You will need to use your own money to pay for the candy you took . . . (or you will need to offer to do some work for the manager to pay the store back for the candy you took). Because you stole some candy, you can't go to any store again for two weeks and you can't have any sweets or desserts of any kind for two weeks either. You will have to show me that I can trust you again."
- "Because you took the videotapes from your aunt and uncle, you will need to apologize to them in person. Also, because you don't have the money to pay them back, you will need to go over to their house and do chores to make up for stealing the tapes. We've decided you need to spend the next four Saturdays helping them around the yard and cleaning the house. I also want you to write a four-page essay about why stealing is wrong and give it to me by Saturday."

Bad Language

Parents will not be able to control all the words their children hear. Unfortunately, children who use bad language and are disrespectful of authority in school often become negative leaders among their peers. Elementary-age children usually know the meaning of vulgar words and other forms of offensive language. Sometimes they experiment with these words out of peer pressure, to fit in with a group, or to call attention to themselves. Sometimes children say words that they know will shock others out of anger, unhappiness, or resentment toward authority. The use of bad language, like sarcasm, can be very provocative to parents and may lead them to immediately punish their child. Although a punishment for using bad language may be justified, if the bad language immediately generates an emotional reaction from the parent, then the parent's reaction can inadvertently reinforce the bad language. The child might find this degree of control over a parent's emotional state too tempting to resist.

A better first step in dealing with bad language is to control your initial emotional reaction long enough to investigate your child's understanding of the words and where he or she learned the bad language. A calm but detailed conversation, although awkward, can reveal important information about your child's understanding, motivation, and source of the bad language. As with the other misbehaviors such as untruthfulness, you should give yourself enough time to prepare for an in-depth conversation about why bad language is not appropriate and a plan for how your child can avoid using such language. This conversation is especially important if the source of the bad language turns out to be a peer who is in a leadership position.

This information can help you assist your child in dealing with peer pressure. You can give your child specific suggestions for the situations he or she is encountering outside the home. Also, by talking with your child first, you may discover more direct action is needed to get to the source of the bad language. For example, you may need to have a meeting with teachers or with other parents. This approach also applies when the source of the bad language is a peer in the neighborhood or even a member of the extended family. As with preschool-age children, parents should tell their children what kind of language they expect and offer acceptable substitute words. If the use of bad language continues, then a system of incentives and negative consequences can be developed for the use of appropriate and inappropriate language.

Examples of parent statements:

- "I want to talk to you about that kind of language. Sometimes when people say those kinds of words to other people, they don't really know what they're saying or it's just a bad habit. But most of the time when people say those kinds of words to other people, they are feeling angry and weak. They're trying to make someone else feel weak or not important or they're just trying to make someone else feel worse than they feel. Some people don't feel good unless they can make other people feel bad. People who do that to other people are only thinking of themselves. There are good ways to let people know when you're angry or upset. Using those words is not a good way to handle being mad."
- "I don't like that word. It's not a polite word. You need to use (substitute word) instead. Please do not say that word again. I think people who use that word aren't using good manners."
- "If you forget our rule about bad language again, you will not be able to play with your friends for two days. I'm warning you, that I'm not going to tolerate that kind of language. You'll be getting some serious consequences if your language doesn't improve."

Untruthfulness

By the age of eight or nine, children know the difference between reality and fiction. Unlike preschoolers, when children of this age are untruthful, they probably know they are not being truthful. Learning to be honest and admit wrongdoing is critical to a child's positive character development. However, elementary-age children are still very concerned about their competency. They can find making mistakes embarrassing or shameful, even if no one else sees the mistake. Children can also be untruthful simply to avoid punishment or chores. The two types of untruthfulness most often encountered are hiding wrongdoing from parents or authority figures and knowingly misrepresenting the facts about a problem situation to make themselves look blameless.

No one likes to be in the wrong and children understandably try to hide wrongdoing from time to time. However, children need to learn to be accountable for their actions. They need to learn to admit wrongdoing and take the consequences. Children are more likely to learn how to face up to their mistakes instead of avoiding the consequences when parents use nonaggressive methods of discipline. These methods respect children's feelings and focus on teaching them how to behave rather than chastising them and focusing on the wrongdoing. Children are less likely to be untruthful when they are not afraid of being humiliated or hurt if their parents learn the truth. Making mistakes becomes a learning experience, though a painful one.

When you know for certain that your child has done something wrong, you should be up front that you know about it. Avoid setting up your child to lie by fishing around or hinting for the child to confess. Get straight to the point in a matter-of-fact way.

Examples of parent statements:

- "I heard from Mrs. Smith that you were using words we don't use in our family when you were over there yesterday."
- "I know you haven't turned in your homework for several days."
- "Don't tell me something that's not true. That will make it hard for me to know the next time whether or not you're telling me the truth."

When you are uncertain about the true facts, you can make it clear that you are more interested in the facts than in blame.

Examples of parent statements:

- "I noticed that you haven't been playing with Tim lately. Has something happened?"
- "You don't seem to have as much homework this week as usual. I'd like to know if there's a problem so I can help you."
- "I hope that you would trust me enough to tell me if you have done something that you shouldn't have."

If you catch your child in an obvious untruth, in addition to giving the child a consequence for the wrongdoing, you should talk privately with him or her about why honesty is so important. Explain that trust is broken when people are dishonest and when two people cannot trust each other, their relationship is damaged. Reading or telling your child a story with a moral about the importance of truthfulness can also be effective in getting this point across. Sometimes children respond well when their parents tell them about a time in their own childhood when they learned why being untruthful is not good. When a child repeatedly lies about wrongdoing, the parent should consider giving a consequence for the lie in addition to a consequence for the wrongdoing. If lying continues to be a problem, consult a professional for advice because lying can become an ingrained habit with serious long-term consequences.

Examples of parent statements:

- "I know you don't want to get in trouble, so it's hard for you to let me know about things you've done that were mistakes. It's very important for me to be able to trust you and for you to be able to trust me. People need to be able to trust each other. People need to know they can count on someone. When you don't tell the truth all the time, I can't be sure when to believe you and when not to believe you, and then I can't trust you. When I can't trust you I can't give you as much freedom, because I won't be able to be sure that you will make good choices. I won't know what you need help with or what I need to do to help you learn how to be safe. I can't help you learn what to do differently the next time if I don't know what you did wrong."

- "What would it be like for you if you couldn't trust me to tell you the truth?" (*Have your child come up with some examples of how it would be bad for him or her if you didn't tell the truth to them. Do not criticize any of your child's answers.*) "That's a good point. What else? . . . That's another good point. You know the most important point for me is that if trust gets broken, it's never the same again. There's always a little bit of a worry about whether or not you can count on someone anymore. If you couldn't be sure if I were going to pick you up after school, every day you'd worry about whether or not I was going to get you and how you'd get home if I didn't."

If your child is being oppositional and not working with you about telling the truth, say that you want her or him to think about it. Say that the two of you will discuss it later when she or he is ready to work with you. Have your child remain in her or his room or other time-out place while considering the behavior. Be prepared to explain the difference between the *social white lie* and a *genuine lie* intended to conceal wrong-doing. A social white lie is to protect someone's feelings or privacy when the truth would serve no useful purpose. The most common example is when people greet each other with, "How's it going?" some say, "Just fine," when life that day is not "just fine."

Application of a Behavior Change Program for Elementary-Age Children

When elementary-age children become untruthful there is usually a pattern to the situations where lying occurs that, when examined, reveals a problem that the child is trying to manage by being untruthful. A situation where a child has developed a pattern of lying to avoid a specific responsibility—schoolwork—was selected for this example. By providing structure, monitoring, and giving incentives for schoolwork performance, the situational factors contributing to lying are changed.

Sample Program to Stop Lying About Schoolwork

As mentioned in chapter 4, a behavior change program should begin with a careful analysis. You should get an idea of the pattern for lying about schoolwork and an idea about why the behavior is emerging now. Having your child define what lying means and how lying effects relationships is very useful. Also, have your child tell you why doing well in school is important. You should also describe not only your values and beliefs about lying, but also why you want your child to be honest with you about schoolwork. Be sure to include both actively telling a lie and hiding truths about schoolwork. Ask your child what changes on your part will help, and be open to any suitable suggestions.

You should also encourage your child to explain why he or she does not do homework and then lies about it. Your child's explanation will help you determine what factors might be contributing to the problem. For example, does the child lie because an undiagnosed learning problem makes the work too hard or because avoiding schoolwork is a symptom of a general avoidance of responsibilities? The explanation often reveals a child's attitude about school, schoolwork, and the child's belief about his or her academic abilities. Knowing your child's attitude will help you and your child design a more effective program and decide on what specific behaviors to target over what length of time. Talking about the problem, possible reasons for it, and solutions helps children acknowledge their role in changing the behavior.

Example of parent statements:

- "You know how you haven't been telling me about your schoolwork? Sometimes you tell me you don't have any and sometimes you tell me you forgot it. Did you realize that not telling me about schoolwork is as much a lie as you telling me you don't have homework when you really do?"
- "Schoolwork is not usually as much fun as playing with your friends, but if you don't learn as much as you can, you won't have as many opportunities to do what you want to do when you're grown-up. Do you have some ideas about why you would try to get out of doing homework? What can I do differently to help you tell me when you have schoolwork?"
- "I know you don't like reading. If you lie to me about your reading assignments, then I can't help you and things just get worse. Even if you lie, reading will not go away, but if you lie, I won't be able to trust you to tell me what you need help with. I won't be able trust you to be responsible. I can't give you more privileges if you're not responsible."
- "I thought we could try a schoolwork chart so you could practice being truthful about your schoolwork. I want to help you practice being able to tell me about your schoolwork."

Once the target behavior is clearly defined and understood by the child, then the program structure can be spelled out. You can give your child tokens or checkmarks on a chart for complying with academic responsibilities and remove the child's usual privileges when he or she hides or lies about schoolwork. Initially, do not involve the teacher unless the avoidance of schoolwork is so serious that the teacher's feedback about assignments is necessary for the program to work.

Work out an exchange system with your child. The elementary-age child is likely to be interested in privileges (extra playtime) as well as more concrete rewards (renting a movie). Decide how many checkmarks or tokens are needed for which specific privileges or rewards. Set the number of checkmarks or tokens needed low enough in the beginning so that your child will most likely earn some rewards. Consider giving a very small reward for each day that your child tells you that schoolwork was assigned on that day and shows you the work to be done. This will help keep your child motivated to follow the program. Use as much social reinforcement as possible each time the desirable behavior occurs. Give your child lavish praise for deciding to solve this problem constructively and learn to face responsibility. See page 153 for a sample of a behavior modification chart designed for this example.

Example of parent statement:

- "Here's your schoolwork chart. Every day that you show me the schoolwork that you have to do, you will get a checkmark. For every piece of work you complete on time, I will give you another checkmark. Here's the list of rewards we came up with and how many checkmarks you need for each one of them. Are you ready to start?"

You may need to structure the environment for your child or provide more direct assistance with schoolwork to help your child complete the work. Make sure the room where your child works is as free from distraction as possible. Consider going to the library for lengthier assignments. Daily rewards for completing schoolwork are effective. Small rewards for reaching halfway points in the homework can also help keep a child on track. Sitting next to your child while she or he does the work can help your child feel less lonely or anxious. Your physical presence can be a reminder to stay on track and not dawdle. If being physically present is not possible, occasionally check in with your child in a supportive way. You may say, "How's it going?" or "Do you need any help?" or other positive comments to show support.

As your child begins to improve, either increase the number of tokens or checkmarks your child needs for rewards, or eliminate some behavior from the chart. As your child consistently tells you about schoolwork and completes it, fade out the token system, but continue with social reinforcers, praise, and attention for being honest about schoolwork and completing it.

Role-Playing to Rehearse and Reinforce Appropriate Behavior

You can make use of your child's growing capacity for abstract reasoning and relativistic thinking by teaching your child to use positive

Behavior change programs help children learn
new behavior in a positive way.

self-talk when she or he feels the urge to avoid schoolwork. You can teach your child to make statements such as:

- "I'll do one more problem before I take a short break."
- "I can finish these problems tonight."
- "I will tell Mom the truth. I will tell Dad the truth. I won't like missing my TV show tonight, but I will tell Mom and Dad that I have homework tonight."
- "I'll just try my best and I won't stop until I have practiced all the spelling words."

Behavior Modification Chart for Schoolwork

date: _____

Schoolwork	Monday	Tuesday	Wednesday	Thursday	Friday	Saturday	Sunday
brings home written assignment							
brings home school supplies and books needed for schoolwork							
finishes work before 8:00 PM							
shows completed work to Mom or Dad							
works in fifteen-minute chunks/no breaks							

CHAPTER 10

You Don't Have
to Be Perfect

Key Ideas

- Relationships are built over time.

- The overall pattern of consistently "good enough" parenting responses is what matters, not isolated events.

Encouragement and Compassion Motivate Children

Children and parents want to love each other. They do not need to be perfect. Each day brings new opportunities to develop and strengthen relationships between family members. Positive interactions build the affection and understanding that allow each of us to tolerate the normal mistakes and imperfections of our loved ones. Understanding and working with the imperfections of both parents and children prepares a child to handle the complexities of relationships beyond the family.

Relationships are built and strengthened through the repeating, day-to-day interactions of our lives. The overall pattern of consistently adequate or "good enough" parenting responses is what matters, not single events. When a parent feels badly about a parenting decision, the parent should use that situation as an opportunity to reflect on what went into that decision and what changes might be made in the future.

In the long run, a child's success depends upon being given the opportunity to learn how to be competent and achieve as well as how to

Success depends upon opportunities for learning.

Keep the big picture in mind when choosing disciplinary methods.

be cooperative with legitimate authority. The encouragement and compassion from legitimate authority is what motivates children to cooperate and succeed.

Having a broad range of disciplinary strategies helps parents be flexible, without being inconsistent. They can fit their methods to their child and to their own values. They are better able to make thoughtful judgments in the face of intense emotions and not act on impulse.

Every child and every family has unique characteristics and values that need to be considered in all parenting decisions. The specific strategies described in this book are only examples used to illustrate how key principles can be applied. You must determine which principles fit your values and then tailor methods to fit your own unique family.

When you keep the big picture of what kind of adult you want your child to be, you already have a basic plan. Fitting and altering specific methods to fit that plan are part of a problem-solving process.

Problem-solving involves educated guesses and trial-and-error learning that are not only unavoidable but necessary. Knowing as much as possible about child development and parenting methods will help you make sound parenting decisions that support the long-term best interests of your child and family.

The following readings are recommended for more comprehensive information on child development and techniques for managing problem behavior in children.

Principles of Behavior Change

Presented below are the technical or scientific definitions of reinforcement and punishment. We usually think of reinforcement as good or pleasant consequences that produce positive results. We usually think of punishment as painful consequences that stop misbehavior. Although this is often the case, technically consequences are judged to be either reinforcing or punishing strictly according to how they affect behavior (or misbehavior). When a consequence increases behavior, it is a reinforcer (for example, peer attention can increase misbehavior). If a consequence decreases behavior, it is considered a punishment even if it is not unpleasant. For example, time-out is technically a reinforcer when the warning or possibility of a time-out works to increase positive behavior. Time-out is technically a punishment when it works to decrease tantrums even though it is not painful or harsh and actually offers children the opportunity to calm themselves down and feel better.

Reinforcement: Positive and Negative

A reinforcer is something that increases or strengthens a behavior or misbehavior.

Positive reinforcement = pleasurable reward

Examples: food, praise, attention, affection, awards, prizes

Negative reinforcement = removal or avoidance of a painful "event" or threat of one

Examples: Adult: *being on time* to work to avoid being fired or reprimanded; *going the speed limit* to avoid a traffic fine;

Child: *remembering* to bring show and tell item to avoid feeling left out or embarrassed.

Punishment: Punishing Event or Penalty

A punishing event is any consequence that decreases a behavior or misbehavior. For example, a parent may experience a child's whining as punishing; children usually find teasing punishing. There are two basic categories of punishment or punishing events:

Application of a negative event (for example, whining, teasing, spanking)

Removal of a positive event (for example, privilege taken away, time-out)

Relationship Between Reinforcement and Punishment		
Positive event	*Application*	*Removal*
	Positive Reinforcement (attention, awards, food, praise, privileges	**Punishment** removal from or of a positive event (privileges taken away, time-out)
Negative event	**Punishment** "aversive control" whining, scolding logical conse- quences, nagging	**Negative Reinforcement** removal or avoidance of negative event (nagging, whining, teasing, anxiety)

References

Bates, L., F. L. Ames, and C. C. Haber. 1989. *Gessell Institute of Child Development Series.* New York: Dell Publishing Co., Inc. (These books cover infancy through 6 years of age.)

Briggs, D. C. 1970. *Your Child's Self-Esteem.* New York: Dolphin Books.

Christopherson, E. R. 1991. Oppositional Behavior in Children. *Pediatric Annals* 20 (5), May, 267–273.

Coie, J. D., and K. F. Lenox 1994. The development of antisocial individuals. *Progress in Experimental Personality and Psycholopathology Research.* 45–72.

Costello, E. J., and M. A. Shugart 1992. Above and below the threshold: Severity of psychiatric symptoms and functional impairmenting pediatric sample. *Pediatrics* 90 (3), September, 359–368.

Dinkmeyer, D. and G. D. McKay 1982. *S.T.E.P.—A Series (Early Childhood, Latency, Adolescence).* Circle Pines, MN: American Guidance Service.

Dreikus, R., and V. Soltz 1964. *Children: The Challenge.* New York: Hawthorn Books, Inc.

Forehand, R. L., and R. J. 1981. *Helping the Noncompliant Child: A Clinician's Guide to Parent Training.* New York: Guilford Press.

Gordon, T. 1975. *P.E.T.: Parent Effectiveness Training*. New York: Wyden Books (hardback), 1970; New American Library (paperback).

Kaplan, L. 1978. *Oneness & Separateness: From Infant to Individual*. New York: Simon & Schuster.

Kanoy, A. E. and C. S. Schroeder 1985. Suggestions to parents about common behavior problems in a pediatric primary care office: Five years of follow-up. Journal of Pediatric Psychology. 10 (1), 15–30.

Kazdin, A. E. and C. Fame 1983. Aggressive behavior and conduct disorder. In R. J. Morris & T. R. Kratochwill (Eds), *The Practice of Child Therapy*. New York: Pergamon Press.

Larzelere, R. E., M. Klein, W. R. Schumm, and W. R. Alibrnado, Jr. 1989. Relations of spanking and other parenting characteristics to self-esteem and perceived fairness of parental discipline. *Psychological Reports*. 64, 1140–1142.

Leshback, S. 1970. Agression. In P. H. Mussen (Ed.), *Manual of Child Psychology*. New York: John Wiley & Sons, Inc. 159–259.

Lewis, R. J., E. L. Dlugokinski, L. M. Caputo, and R. B. Griffin 1988. Children at risk for emotional disorders: Risk and resource dimensions. *Clinical Psychology Review*. 8, 417–440.

McCormick, M. D. and F. Kenelm 1992. Attitudes of Primary Care Physicians Toward Corporal Punishment. *JAMA*, 267 (23), June 17, 3161–3165.

Miller, G. E., L. H. London, and R. J. Prinz 1991. Understanding and treating serious childhood behavior disorders. *Family and Community Health*. 14 (3), 33–41.

Orentlicher, D. 1992. From the office of the general counsel: Corporal Punishment in the Schools. *JAMA*. 267 (23), June, 17.

Patterson, G. 1976. *Living with Children*. Champaign, IL: Research Press.

Patterson, G. 1990. *Depression and Aggression in Family Interaction*. New York: Lawrence Erlbaum Associates.

Patterson G. 1989. A developmental perspective on antisocial behavior. *American Psychologist.* 44 (2), 329–35.

Piaget, J. Piaget's theory. In P. H. Mussen (Ed.), *Manual of Child Psychology.* New York: John Wiley & Sons, Inc. 703–732.

Rey, J. M. 1993. Oppositional Defiant Disorder. *American Journal of Psychiatry.* 150 (12), December, 1769–1778.

Webster-Stratton, C. 1990. Enhancing the effectiveness of self-administered video-tape parent training for families with conduct-problem children. *Journal of Abnormal Child Psychology.* 18 (5), 479–492.

Child Behavior Checklists:

Achenback, T. M. and C. S. Edelbrock 1979. The Child Behavioral Profile: II, boys 12–16, girls ages 6–11 and 12–16. *Journal of Consulting and Clinical Psychology.* 47, 223–233.

Robinson, E. A., S. M. Eyberg, and A. W. 1980. The standardization of an inventory of child conduct problem behaviors. *Journal of Clinical Child Psychology.* 9, 22–29.

Goyette, H. C. K. Conners, and R. F. Ulrich 1978. Normative data on the revised Conners Parent and Teacher Rating Scales. *Journal of Abnormal Child Psychology.* 6, 221–236.

Quay, H. C. 1983. A dimensional approach to behavior disorder. *School Psychology Review.* 12, 244–249.

Vineland Adaptive Behavior Scale. Available through American Guidance Service, Inc. 4201 Woodland Road, Circle Pines, MN 55014-1796.

Other New Harbinger Self-Help Titles

When Anger Hurts Your Kids, $12.95
The Addiction Workbook, $17.95
The Mother's Survival Guide to Recover, $12.95
The Chronic Pain Control Workbook, Second Edition, $17.95
Fibromyalgia & Chronic Myofacial Pain Sybndrome, $19.95
Diagnosis and Treatment of Sociopaths, $44.95
Flying Without Fear, $12.95
Kid Cooperation: How to Stop Yelling, Nagging & Pleading and Get Kids to Cooperate, $12.95
The Stop Smoking Workbook: Your Guide to Healthy Quitting, $17.95
Conquering Carpal Tunnel Syndrome and Other Repetitive Strain Injuries, $17.95
The Tao of Conversation, $12.95
Wellness at Work: Building Resilience for Job Stress, $17.95
What Your Doctor Can't Tell You About Cosmetic Surgery, $13.95
An End of Panic: Breakthrough Techniques for Overcoming Panic Disorder, $17.95
On the Clients Path: A Manual for the Practice of Solution-Focused Therapy, $39.95
Living Without Procrastination: How to Stop Postponing Your Life, $12.95
Goodbye Mother, Hello Woman: Reweaving the Daughter Mother Relationship, $14.95
Letting Go of Anger: The 10 Most Common Anger Styles and What to Do About Them, $12.95
Messages: The Communication Skills Workbook, Second Edition, $13.95
Coping With Chronic Fatigue Syndrome: Nine Things You Can Do, $12.95
The Anxiety & Phobia Workbook, Second Edition, $17.95
Thueson's Guide to Over-The Counter Drugs, $13.95
Natural Women's Health: A Guide to Healthy Living for Women of Any Age, $13.95
I'd Rather Be Married: Finding Your Future Spouse, $13.95
The Relaxation & Stress Reduction Workbook, Fourth Edition, $17.95
Living Without Depression & Manic Depression: A Workbook for Maintaining Mood Stability, $17.95
Belonging: A Guide to Overcoming Loneliness, $13.95
Coping With Schizophrenia: A Guide For Families, $13.95
Visualization for Change, Second Edition, $13.95
Postpartum Survival Guide, $13.95
Angry All The Time: An Emergency Guide to Anger Control, $12.95
Couple Skills: Making Your Relationship Work, $13.95
Handbook of Clinical Psychopharmacology for Therapists, $39.95
The Warrior's Journey Home: Healing Men, Healing the Planet, $13.95
Weight Loss Through Persistence, $13.95
Post-Traumatic Stress Disorder: A Complete Treatment Guide, $39.95
Stepfamily Realities: How to Overcome Difficulties and Have a Happy Family, $13.95
Leaving the Fold: A Guide for Former Fundamentalists and Others Leaving Their Religion, $13.95
Father-Son Healing: An Adult Son's Guide, $12.95
The Chemotherapy Survival Guide, $11.95
Your Family/Your Self: How to Analyze Your Family System, $12.95
Being a Man: A Guide to the New Masculinity, $12.95
The Deadly Diet, Second Edition: Recovering from Anorexia & Bulimia, $13.95
Last Touch: Preparing for a Parent's Death, $11.95
Consuming Passions: Help for Compulsive Shoppers, $11.95
Self-Esteem, Second Edition, $13.95
I Can't Get Over It, A Handbook for Trauma Survivors, $13.95
Concerned Intervention, When Your Loved One Won't Quit Alcohol or Drugs, $11.95
Dying of Embarrassment: Help for Social Anxiety and Social Phobia, $12.95
The Depression Workbook: Living With Depression and Manic Depression, $17.95
The Marriage Bed: Renewing Love, Friendship, Trust, and Romance, $11.95
Focal Group Psychotherapy: For Mental Health Professionals, $44.95
Hot Water Therapy: Save Your Back, Neck & Shoulders in 10 Minutes a Day $11.95
Prisoners of Belief: Exposing & Changing Beliefs that Control Your Life, $12.95
Be Sick Well: A Healthy Approach to Chronic Illness, $11.95
Men & Grief: A Guide for Men Surviving the Death of a Loved One., $13.95
When the Bough Breaks: A Helping Guide for Parents of Sexually Abused Childern, $11.95
Love Addiction: A Guide to Emotional Independence, $12.95
When Once Is Not Enough: Help for Obsessive Compulsives, $13.95
The New Three Minute Meditator, $12.95
Getting to Sleep, $12.95
Beyond Grief: A Guide for Recovering from the Death of a Loved One, $13.95
Leader's Guide to the Relaxation & Stress Reduction Workbook, Fourth Edition, $19.95
The Divorce Book, $13.95
Hypnosis for Change: A Manual of Proven Techniques, 2nd Edition, $13.95
When Anger Hurts, $13.95
Free of the Shadows: Recovering from Sexual Violence, $12.95
Lifetime Weight Control, $11.95
Love and Renewal: A Couple's Guide to Commitment, $13.95

Call **toll free, 1-800-748-6273**, to order. Have your Visa or Mastercard number ready. Or send a check for the titles you want to New Harbinger Publications, Inc., 5674 Shattuck Ave., Oakland, CA 94609. Include $3.80 for the first book and 75¢ for each additional book, to cover shipping and handling. (California residents please include appropriate sales tax.) Allow four to six weeks for delivery.

Prices subject to change without notice.